WHO *more than* WISHED YOU WERE DEAD?

What Did You Do Before Dying?

Why Did You Die in the Park?

A Marge Christensen Mystery

WHO *more than* WISHED
YOU WERE DEAD?

To Mystery Readers Everywhere!

Patricia K. Batta

PATRICIA K. BATTA

LILLIMAR PUBLISHING
TRAVERSE CITY, MICHIGAN

Lillimar Publishing
www.lillimarpublishing.com

Batta, Patricia K.
Who more than wished you were dead? : a Marge Christensen mystery /
Patricia K. Batta — Traverse City, Mich. : Lillimar Publishing, c2010.
p. ; cm.
ISBN: 978-0-9797883-4-5

1. Christensen, Marge (Fictitious character)—Fiction. 2. Widows—Fiction.
3. Abused wives—Fiction. 4. Abusive men—Fiction.
5. Ocean Shores (Wash.)—Fiction. 6. Mystery fiction.

PS3602.A898 W46 2008   2010933739
813/.6—dc22   1010

Printed in the United States of America
10 9 8 7 6 5 4 3 2 1

COVER & INTERIOR DESIGN BY TO THE POINT SOLUTIONS
www.tothepointsolutions.com

This is a work of fiction. Names, characters, places, and incidents either are the product of the author's imagination or are used fictitiously, and any resemblance to actual persons, living or dead, businesses, companies, events, or locales is entirely coincidental.

WHO *more than* WISHED
YOU WERE DEAD?

ONE

～

"AM I EVER READY for this!" Marge said as she parked the blue Honda wagon in the resort's lot on Friday afternoon. As the result of some unspecified job-related award that her son, Robert, had earned, she had a whole glorious week ahead of her at the shore. A week of peace. She would have to figure out some way to celebrate her son's achievement and to properly thank him for his generosity.

In the several years since her husband, Gene, died, she had been too busy with work, money concerns, and family problems to think about taking a vacation. A deep cleansing breath, exhaled slowly, helped rid her of driving tensions and everyday worries that had invaded her solitary journey.

Fortunately, the torrential rain that had slowed her drive to a snail's pace until she was halfway between Aberdeen and Ocean Shores had let up before she reached the short stretch of switchbacks near the end of her trip. The anticipated two-and-a-half-hour drive to Mariner Village—which was the farthest she had ever driven by herself—had turned into an almost-four-hour ordeal.

Stepping out of the car into the November chill, Marge reached high to stretch stiff lower-back muscles. She ran a hand through her riotous mass of short auburn curls. Given the shore's damp weather, she expected every day here would be a bad hair day.

A slow smile eased the tightness around her eyes. She had done it. One more thing she had handled alone. Driving a long distance, even in western Washington's unpredictable November weather, was another pleasure she wouldn't have to give up because she was a widow. Or, worse, depend on her children to do for her.

A blast of cold wind whistled through the parking lot, biting through her shirt and lifting a few errant leaves. It left her refreshed but shivering. Marge scurried into the resort office to check in for herself, Robert, and her daughter, Kate. And Robert's date, of course. A frown creased her forehead. So much for forgetting about family problems. Robert hadn't told her until this morning that he was bringing a guest; a woman neither she nor Kate had met. Was that what this vacation was really about—introducing his new love interest into the family?

"Is something wrong?"

Startled, Marge glanced up to see a plump face framed by flyaway blonde curls.

"No, I'm sorry. I guess I didn't leave all of my cares behind yet."

The woman laughed and held out her hand. "Hello, I'm Jane, the resort manager. Let's get you checked in so you can start to relax."

"I hope you can order up some sun," Marge said when

she had completed the paperwork. "Especially for the weekend, since my children will only be here for two nights."

"The weather report does say sun tomorrow," said Jane. Marge only had to look at Jane's sunny face to feel warmth. "You should have a nice weekend, but around here we can't predict far enough ahead to make any guesses about the rest of your stay."

"Do we have a view of the ocean from our unit?" Marge asked.

"Yes. The developers were fortunate to get a nice, high piece of land close to the jetty for the resort," Jane said. "From the third floor, where your room is, you have a good view of the beach and the surf. We lost half our frontage to a huge storm a couple of years ago, which is why there is now a steep drop to the beach. Find the path and you will be able to make your way down." Her clear-blue eyes twinkled. "Nothing as bad as that storm is forecast for *your* week, so enjoy your stay."

Back out on the cold, Marge grabbed a cart from a nook beside the entry and loaded it with her suitcase, painting supplies, and the groceries she had brought from home and purchased at the IGA on her way through town. An elevator centered between banks of condos took her to the third floor, where she wheeled the cart to their assigned unit. She stowed the groceries, returned the cart, and heated water in a handy teakettle for a mug of peppermint tea before surveying the surprisingly complete kitchen. Salt, pepper, and a small array of spices in the cupboard would make cooking easy; dishwashing and laundry detergent were under the sink; and a starter supply of coffee, sugar, and creamer beside the coffee maker promised the comfort of a warm morning drink.

Wrapping her hands around the mug to take advantage of its warmth, Marge wandered through the condo. A sofa and two chairs were arranged to best take advantage of the gas fireplace, the view out the deck slider doors, and a television set in the wall. Color-coordinated artificial flower arrangements on the coffee table and dining table, as well as tasteful artwork on the walls, gave the room a finished look. More televisions in the two bedrooms, a DVD player, and a stereo/CD system provided for rainy-day entertainment. She hadn't expected it to be so completely and tastefully furnished.

"So, where are we all going to sleep?" she murmured as she finished her inspection. "Even though Robert is an adult . . . while under my roof . . ." She wavered. This wasn't her roof. In a way, it was his. Still, she thought, nodding at her tea for emphasis, while under the same roof he would follow her rules, as outdated as they might seem to him. She hadn't figured out what she would do if he refused. Go home? That would make a good threat. Robert wouldn't want her to leave after he had insisted she come.

Pulling on a sweatshirt, Marge stepped onto the roomy deck, noting the gas grill nestled in one corner. It was barely five o'clock, but everything was beginning to look dim under the looming clouds. White crests rose before smashing back into the slate-gray ocean; their ferocity took her breath away. As a bracing cold wind cleared the last remnants of tension from her body, she closed her eyes against an unexpected wave of aloneness. Not loneliness exactly, but an aloneness that even now, several years after being thrust unexpectedly into widowhood, returned to surprise her with a confused emptiness. She shook herself to dispel the feeling and opened her eyes. Two couples, bundled in jackets against the damp chill, fought the wind to stay on a path leading from the resort through dune grass and brush that extended out to the edge of the cliff. Once there, they stopped for several minutes. Evidently thinking better of continuing down the embankment, they turned and made their way back to the resort. Marge shivered at the idea of standing in this wind at the top of that embankment, the other side of which appeared to be a sheer drop to the beach.

Even with approaching darkness the beach showed signs of activity, probably because most people would have arrived today and been impatient to start their vacations. To her left, in the distance, she could see the end of an outcropping of huge boulders which had to be the jetty that separated Grays Harbor Bay from the ocean. Six people trudged from that direction into the wind. A tall, well-muscled man, wearing only shorts and a t-shirt, took off at a jog. He turned and waved tauntingly to the rest of his group; three men who wore more appropriate jeans and sweatshirts and two women in sweat suits, one pink and one blue. The he-man type, Marge thought with distaste as her eyes followed the man in the lead. She frowned, lifted her hand, and lightly slapped her jaw. Struggling to learn to be less judgmental, this was her gentle reminder when she slipped. After all, she couldn't know anything about that man and had no business forming an opinion on the basis of his clothing choice, even if she did consider it foolish.

The woman in pink wore a headband; she lagged behind the others. If the wind grew any stronger, she might end up walking in place. As Marge watched, the four others stopped and turned, taking a break from facing the wind while waiting for the slowpoke to catch up. Only the leader jogged on, apparently oblivious to her discomfort. Soon after the woman caught up to the others, the three men walked ahead again. The woman in blue walked slower and appeared to be urging her companion to walk faster. The lady in pink had her head down and didn't seem to respond. The lady in blue finally gave up and ran ahead to join the men.

Marge blinked as everyone but the woman in pink disappeared from view. She couldn't help but wonder about the nuances of that scene. Had pink sweats been ill and was still weak? If so, why didn't anyone stay with her? She stopped the hand that was about to slap her jaw again. No, she wasn't being judgmental, she was being nosy, another frequent failing. She needed a different reminder for that, like maybe pinching her nose. These people had nothing to do with her and she had no need to know their affairs. She shook off the last remnants of aloneness and went inside the condo.

Kate breezed in at six, carrying a bag of groceries and a six-pack of beer. "You made good time!" Marge exclaimed. She hadn't expected Kate until nearly nine, since she often worked late at her Seattle law office.

"I left work early," Kate said. "And I took the ferry from downtown Seattle to Bremerton. I would have arrived sooner, but I didn't have any books to bring and I didn't know what was available here, so I took time to find a bookstore in Bremerton. When I got to Ocean Shores, I decided to stop at the IGA to stock up on some junk food you might not have thought of." Her green eyes sparkled. Marge noted once again how much more startling those eyes were with the dark-brown hair and olive-toned skin Kate had inherited from her father.

"Your ferry ride couldn't have been that much fun in the rain," Marge said as she helped Kate unload chips and dip, popcorn, snack bars, energy drinks, and beer.

"Yeah, but that's just it," Kate said. "I got on the ferry and didn't have to worry about the rain or the rush hour traffic. I enjoyed a beer in the warmth of the cabin. And, the rain let up by the time I started driving."

"After the beer," Marge said.

Kate laughed, wiggled her brows, and pulled a beer off the six-pack. It reminded Marge of Kate's teenage years, when she deliberately did whatever she knew Marge didn't want her to do. Marge had to grin in acknowledgement of the rebuke, burying the tiny niggle of concern that her daughter was getting too old for some of the choices she made.

Robert and Ruthie arrived about seven. Robert also had Gene's coloring, including his brown eyes, but he inherited his height and athletic build from Marge's father.

Marge studied Ruthie, trying not to be obvious. Robert had not rushed into dating after his divorce from Caroline last year. This girl appeared to be quite different; a bit younger than Robert's twenty-nine years, with a pleasantly round face, fluffy dark-blonde hair pulled back in a pony tail, and soft hazel eyes. In fact, she had a look of pillowy softness all about her. Robert apparently didn't want to make the mistake of replacing his ex-wife with another hard-driving businesswoman.

Marge cringed. Her heart felt hollow every time she thought of Caroline aborting what would have been Marge's first grandchild and the subsequent breakup of Robert and Caroline's marriage. She knew she had to find it in her heart to forgive and not judge Caroline for a decision her daughter-in-law made in a situation Marge had never had to deal with—the same decision, she later discovered, also made by a majority of women when they learned the child they carried had Down's syndrome. Marge hadn't gotten there yet.

By the time they were ready to think about dinner, the ocean had long since disappeared into a dark night and the wind had picked up to such ferocity Marge abandoned the idea of using the gas grill. Robert and Kate each took a can of beer and Ruthie drank a wine cooler she and Robert had brought, along with another assortment of snack food. The kids must think they needed to provide against a weekend of mother making them eat their vegetables.

Marge poured herself a glass of cabernet, slapped the hamburger patties on the broiling pan, and readied the buns to toast in the oven while Kate arranged lettuce, tomato, and cheese on a plate. Store-bought potato salad and fresh fruit completed the meal.

"Robert, I saw a friend of yours on the ferry," Kate said between bites. "At least, she said she knew you. She was with a group staying down the road at the Point Brown Resort."

"Did you get her name?" Robert's voice seemed guarded.

Marge glanced at him, but his eyes were on his food. His eyes always gave him away when he wasn't being entirely truthful. Had he known this friend was coming to Ocean Shores? If so, why hide it?

"Hillary something," Kate said.

"Carlson," Robert supplied, his brows knitting as if surprised, but his eyes still concealed. "Hillary Carlson. Before she married, she worked in the credit department of the store where Caroline is a buyer. She quit working after marriage, since that's what Craig, her husband, wanted. She and Caroline didn't stay in touch but I've talked to Hillary off and on."

And how had that come about? Marge wondered. When Robert finally glanced up, she caught a look she couldn't quite decipher. Perhaps he was thinking of the contrast with Caroline, who thought it a weakness to even consider letting her husband decide whether she should do something.

"Did she seem all right?" Robert asked.

"Yeah, I guess. Maybe a little quiet, but I figured that's her nature."

"It is now," Robert said. Marge sensed hardness behind the words. She looked again at Robert, hoping for an explanation, but his brow was furrowed in a way that told Marge he had no more to say on the subject. If the sharp glance that Ruthie sent his way was any indication, she would also have liked to hear some elaboration of Robert's connection with Hillary Carlson.

"So, Robert, what wonders did you achieve at work that made them reward you with this fantastic condo for a week?" Kate asked.

Robert straightened and put a smile on his face. "It is pretty neat, isn't it?" he said. "My achievements weren't so great that we got it in good weather, though. Or even when the workload was light enough so I could take a week off. Mom, did you find someone to come and join you after we go back to work on Monday?"

Marge noted that he hadn't answered Kate's question. Something was going on. She found herself beginning to strategize about how she was going to find out what it was. "You remember my friend Melissa, the real estate agent who sold our house? She plans to take a few days off and join me. And, I won't mind if I have some alone time. It will help me get some paintings done for my Christmas exhibit at the shop. But, if Melissa can delay showing property for a few days, she will stay the rest of the week." She turned to Ruthie. "I'm glad you could come, too. I hope you enjoy the ocean as much as we do."

"Oh, yes! I think it's absolutelytotallywonderful," Ruthie gushed, making it sound like one word. She tipped her head to peer at Robert, as if gauging his reaction. He had the good sense to look uncomfortable at her effusiveness. Marge turned away in time to catch Kate pantomime sticking two fingers down her throat. With a scowl and a cough, Marge tried to cover up the laugh that threatened to escape.

"Anybody want to go bar hopping in beautiful down-town Ocean Shores?" Kate asked.

"Grow up, Kate," Robert said. "We're all tired and we've already had enough to drink."

Kate raised an eyebrow and gazed at his single beer with the you've-got-to-be-kidding look she had mastered when they both lived at home. She didn't pursue it, though. That was probably wise, since Robert would have been quick to point out the several beers she had downed. They opted for a short walk on the parking lot side of the resort which was protected from the worst of the wind by the buildings.

"Why don't you take the master bedroom, Mom?" Robert suggested when they returned to the condo. "The girls can take the twin beds in the other bedroom and I'll sleep on the Murphy bed in the living room."

Wow, Marge thought. So much for her planned threat to go home if he didn't agree to that exact arrangement. Why was he being so amenable? He cared enough about Ruthie to bring her to the shore with him, into the bosom of his family so to speak, but he wasn't on intimate terms with her? Well, she could hope that. A more likely explanation was he knew how Marge felt and didn't want to upset her. Whatever, Marge gave a quick prayer of thanks that it was so easy.

"I know how you feel about these things, Mom, and this week is for you," Robert explained, as if reading her thoughts. "I want you to be comfortable." Ruthie and Kate agreed to the arrangement after a stunned silence. Whatever the reason, Marge was relieved and happy to ensconce herself in the luxury of the master bedroom with her book. She heard Robert on his cell phone for some time, followed by the sound of the living room TV, long after Ruthie and Kate stopped talking in the other bedroom.

Saturday morning Marge rose at six, intending to enjoy a solitary cup of coffee before going for a walk on the beach. Robert was already up and preparing the coffee.

"Good morning. When did you become such an early riser?" she asked.

"A habit left over from my married days," he said.

"Caroline had little use for what she called 'slug-a-beds.' I thought I'd go for a run. I want to get back in shape. I haven't done much of anything for the last few months."

They both stepped out on the deck into a refreshing breeze to sip their coffee. The air was clear and cloudless, stars still visible in the slowly brightening sky. Whitecaps on the now light-gray ocean appeared to fold over gently, but the resulting whoosh and the surge of water onto the beach exposed the power beneath them.

After finishing their coffee, they made their way through the brush on the same uneven path Marge had seen the couples use last night. When they reached the end of the path, they discovered that frequent use had provided an incline of soft yellow sand that angled down the sheer cliff. They slipped and slid to get to the bottom, where they had to trudge through an expanse of equally loose sand before reaching ground that grew firmer as they approached the ocean. Once on firm ground, they turned right and settled into a brisk walk. Robert stayed with Marge a few minutes before giving her a wave and jogging ahead.

On the lookout for interesting shells, Marge kept her eyes on the sand in front of her. She didn't see any whole ones, and not many fragments either. Her seven young art students would be heartbroken if she didn't return with some seashells for them. She'd have to ask at the desk where she could find a good selection. Maybe on the Grays Harbor Bay side of the peninsula.

When she looked up, she discovered she was about to plough into Robert, who had stopped to talk with someone. Marge moved around him, recognizing the pink sweats and headband of the woman who had lagged behind the rest of her friends on the beach last night. The two were deep in conversation, which stopped as soon as they saw Marge. Sadness seemed to envelop the woman, her dark-blue eyes mournful and her full mouth turned down. Even her ash-blonde hair looked limp. She was tall and willowy, but so thin that this morning's breeze, not nearly as robust as last night's gale, appeared strong enough to blow her away.

Robert broke the silence. "Mom, this is Hillary Carlson."

"Hello. Nice to meet you. What brings you to Ocean Shores?" Marge asked.

"My husband and three of his coworkers are staying at a condo owned by their company. My husband was promoted to supervisor and he'll spend the week brainstorming with his team. I'm the only wife along, although there is also one husband." The words were spoken in such a hushed voice Marge had to strain to hear.

"Craig jogged so far ahead that Hillary decided to return to Point Brown," Robert said. "I'm going with her. Don't wait breakfast for me; I don't know how long I'll be."

Marge walked on into the wind, its chill biting at her nose and cheeks, worry eating at her. Hillary and her look of melancholy aroused the "nosiness" she was trying to tame, causing Marge to pinch her cold nose, as well as some judgmental feelings about pulling oneself together, for which she slapped her jaw. But mainly she was curious about why Robert appeared to be so close to a former friend of Caroline's. And how . . . why . . . he happened to arrange a weekend at the beach at the same time as she.

After fifteen minutes, Marge gratefully put her back to the wind for the return trek to the condo. More comfortable now, she was able to smile at the seagulls scattering along the beach at her approach and admire the driftwood, bleached white by the sun and smoothed by wind and water. When she had nearly reached the path going up to the condo she spotted a huge log nestled into an indentation in the cliff. She wondered at the force of nature that could push such a heavy burden so far from the water's edge.

Slogging through the loose sand to get to the log, she looked behind it. She could imagine small children climbing over and around it, creating their own little nook between the log and the cliff. It was so sheltered; anyone sitting back here would be invisible to those on the beach. Still smiling, she continued to the path and clambered up the embankment. She arrived at the condo to find Kate popping blueberry waffles into the toaster.

Ruthie looked distinctly forlorn to find herself alone having breakfast with Robert's sister and mother.

"Did you sleep well?" Marge asked.

"Yes."

Marge glanced at Kate.

"How did you meet Robert?" Kate asked.

"At a party," Ruthie said.

Well, Marge thought, evidently no one ever taught this girl that if you want to get a guy you should be nice to his mother and sister. Of course, she didn't really miss the gushing that took place when Robert was around. No one had told Caroline about being nice, either, but that hadn't stopped Robert from marrying her. Glancing at Ruthie, she inwardly cringed. As little as she knew about this girl, she found herself hoping history wouldn't repeat itself.

After breakfast, Ruthie gazed down at the pool and hot tub surrounded by a Plexiglas fence. The pool was covered, and would be until April according to the information book, but the hot tub opened at nine.

"I wish I had known there was a hot tub, and that Robert would abandon me," Ruthie moaned. "I would have brought my bathing suit."

"You can probably buy one," Kate said. "They may even have them at the office."

"Yeah, but it wouldn't be worth it. We're leaving tomorrow. I suppose Robert does plan to come back and spend *some* time with me." With a pout she grabbed the remote and plopped down in front of the television.

Marge bundled up to sit on the deck with her sketchpad and watercolor pencils, doodling different scenes and trying to decide what to paint first. Kate was ready to take a walk on the beach when Robert returned.

"We've got a date for lunch," he announced. "We're meeting Hillary's group at Alec's by the Sea at twelve-thirty."

"Oh, what fun," Ruthie cried, jumping up, suddenly full of animation.

Kate glared. "Where do you get off making plans for me?" she asked.

"You have something better to do?" Robert countered.

"Children, children," Marge said, laughing at the siblings squabble, as she joined them inside the condo. When she saw Kate stick out her tongue at Robert before leaving for her walk she felt the clock slip backward in time.

"Seriously, though, Robert, why don't you young people go and enjoy yourselves and I'll stay here and sketch?"

"No, Mom. You're not getting out of it that easily. Besides, some of these 'young people' are at least as old as you."

Marge grabbed her back and bent over. "Okay, Sonny, you twisted my arm," she croaked.

Robert, as if trying to make up for his neglect, offered to take Ruthie for a drive around the peninsula. Marge went out to sit on the embankment with her sketchpad and watercolor pencils.

After she had settled in, the man in shorts and a t-shirt jogged past, heading to her left, toward the jetty. If that was Craig Carlson completing his morning jog, it had been a long one, Marge thought. Would he agree to the lunch date the rest of the group had evidently made?

With her fingers flying fast, she caught his long stride and the jut of his chin on her pad. As he passed directly in front of her, he glanced up but showed no signs of seeing her. She could make out the narrowed concentration of his eyes, but not the color. Brown, she determined, to go with the dark-brown hair that was straight and artfully cut and kept long around his ears.

Marge decided that as she worked on sketches, she would draw people as true to life as possible. As she was finishing any paintings for display, she would make sure no one could be identified. Flipping the pages, Marge quickly sketched the changing scene as the jogger continued farther down the beach.

He had gone a short distance past Marge when Hillary, in her pink sweat suit, appeared on Marge's right and came charging towards him. Hillary called out. While the wind made it impossible for Marge to hear her words, it seemed to carry them to the man. He stopped, turned, and stepped back a pace or two as if surprised. Marge frowned. Hillary had gone back to the condo with Robert, too tired to go on. She looked different now. Her back to Marge, Hillary stood rigid with her hands on her hips and her head tilted up toward the face of the man Marge presumed to be her husband. Marge caught her in a few quick strokes of the watercolor pencil before Hillary suddenly shoved the man in the chest, turned, and walked away rapidly, moving at an angle toward the ocean and away from the jetty. Her face still wasn't visible, partly because she wore a hat that hid more of her features than the headband had earlier and partly because of the direction in which she walked. Marge shook her head. Even though Hillary had initiated the exchange, it now seemed she was anxious to get away from the man.

He stood for a moment staring after her. Marge could see a frown furrowing his brow. When he turned and continued jogging toward the jetty Marge looked the other way. Where was Hillary going? With a glance back over her shoulder, as if to be sure Craig was out of sight, Hillary cut back toward the embankment and clambered up it without the benefit of the worn path. She appeared to be headed to the parking lot of another building.

Marge stopped drawing as she tried to make sense of it. Had Hillary gone to her condo at Point Brown Resort with Robert and, after Robert left, driven half a mile in order to return to the beach and wait to confront Craig before he got to the condo? Why would she do that? And where had she found the energy?

Marge took a deep breath, shook her head, and pinched her nose. She was going to have an awfully red nose if she kept this up. It really, truly, was none of her business.

Barely aware of the time passing or the chill creeping through her, Marge concentrated on her work. The main activity at this end of the beach was kite flying, and the sky was full of colorful swooping and soaring shapes, moving so fast in the wind that Marge had a hard time capturing them.

Turning in response to a shout, Marge was surprised to see Robert halfway down the path, waving both hands over his head. She glanced at her watch and jumped up. How did it get to be almost noon? A growing sense of anticipation added lightness to her step as she hurried back to the condo. Perhaps she would learn something over lunch about this overbearing Craig Carlson. Perhaps by the time they returned to the condo she would have some understanding of wimpy Hillary's attraction for Robert.

Or perhaps she would have to pinch her nose until she looked like Rudolph.

TWO

⌒

ROBERT, IN HIS SELF-APPOINTED role as guardian of the females, insisted on driving the five miles to Ocean Shores' city center. That was fine with Marge. It gave her time to appreciate the various shapes of the houses. Some had a gazebo type cupola perched above the main structure, with a stairway stretched up like a goose neck, to achieve the maximum view. And many looked aged as a result of the constant exposure to harsh weather. Marge's fingers itched to start putting the intriguing structures on paper.

At Chance a La Mer, they turned right, away from the ocean. Marge noted a holiday bazaar in progress at the Civic Center. Crossing Brown's Point Road and passing the grocery store, they arrived at Alec's by the Sea.

"Perhaps more accurately known as Alec's no more than a mile from the sea," Kate commented.

The Point Brown contingent was already seated when

17

the hostess ushered them through the restaurant into a side room. "How nice this room was available," Marge said.

The men stood and Robert introduced his family. The man Marge had seen on the beach did the introductions for his group.

"I'm Craig Carlson and this is my wife, Hillary," he said. His eyes were, indeed, brown. Hillary had once again taken on the appearance of a wet dishrag. "My coworker Anne Jacobs, and her husband, John," Craig continued.

Anne was about Hillary's height and almost as slender, but long, smooth muscles kept her from looking as gaunt as Hillary. She had carroty red hair and sharp blue eyes, while John had dark hair and brown eyes. They appeared to be slightly younger than Hillary and Craig.

"And two other coworkers, Richard Wilson and Andrew Barnes."

Aha, these were the older ones Robert had referred to. Richard was as tall as Craig and had the well-developed muscles of a man who worked out; he was a good ten years older than the others. Andrew, lean and sinewy, was Marge's age or more. As they circled around the table meeting each other, Marge's dislike of the domineering Craig Carlson intensified. At the same time, she found Hillary's attention-seeking self-pity irritating. Mentally she gave herself a slap on the chin. How could she be irritated at someone so obviously in misery, especially when its cause was an overbearing man Marge disliked at first sight? While John sat back nursing a beer, Anne acted as hostess to the group. Marge frowned. If they needed a hostess, wasn't that Hillary's job? When they were all seated, Marge found herself next to Andrew Barnes with Kate beside Richard. How had that happened?

"Don't worry, Richard is not predatory," Andrew said quietly into her ear. Marge started, suddenly aware she had been staring at Richard and Kate.

"Are you sure he's the one who worries me?" she countered.

He laughed. "Perhaps I should ask if Kate is predatory."

Marge cocked her head for a moment. "Probably." she said. She had never thought of her daughter as predatory, but she was sure that if Kate wanted something she would go for it whether or not it was politically or socially correct. "Does Richard need protecting?"

It was Andrew's turn to cock his head. Marge couldn't help admiring the unstudied look of his trim sand-brown hair. It was comforting that he had not found it necessary to hide the inroads of gray at the temples. His muted green eyes took on a pensive look as he peered at Richard. "I doubt it. Though he's borne his share of disappointment lately, he should know how to handle whatever comes along." He turned to give his full attention to Marge. "I, on the other hand, am an innocent and need tender loving care."

The words, the teasing green eyes, and the open face of the man beside her made Marge stiffen and lose her train of thought. Her face warmed and she knew that meant her fair, freckled complexion glowed red. She looked away, took a deep breath, and forced her thoughts back to the conversation.

"Richard's disappointment?" she choked.

"Ah, yes. He was in line for the promotion that went to the much younger Craig. Chances are, once passed over, he'll be passed over for the remainder of his career."

"I'm surprised he was willing to spend the week in the same condo with Craig."

"He doesn't have any choice. Craig is his boss now. Can you imagine how difficult Craig could make Richard's life if he decided Richard was no longer a team player?"

"And you? Is Craig your boss, too? And Anne's?"

Andrew's voice was tight when he replied, "No, not

mine, thank God. Yes, Anne also works for him. Craig and I are now both directors, but Craig is starting up a new unit and this trip is for his staff to solidify it and to plan for the coming months. It will be decidedly one-sided brainstorming with Craig in charge."

"But—you also have to be a team player?" Marge looked at Craig. He leaned back, regaling his end of the table with some story while gesturing broadly with his hands. The picture of confidence. Isn't that what it took to be a leader?

"We'll see. I'm along to lend my experience to a novice director—as if he will take it," Andrew said with a wry grin.

Watching Craig work the table, Marge's dislike intensified still more. Automatically, but without the repentance that should go with it, she slapped her chin. Giving Andrew a grin and shrug of the shoulders in answer to his quizzical look, she returned to her perusal of the table.

Ruthie seemed to be hanging on Craig's every word while Kate had turned slightly toward Richard, neatly presenting her back to Craig. Good for you, my girl, Marge thought. She looked at Robert to see how he was taking Ruthie's defection only to find him with his head close to Hillary's; the concentration on his face seemed to respond to her wide-eyed supplication. Marge frowned. Who had defected first? Turning back to Andrew, she found him studying her, his eyes crinkled up in a smile, as if they were sharing a secret joke.

"Better than a soap opera, isn't it?"

"It raises more questions than it answers," Marge replied. She ignored the puzzlement in Andrew's eyes and busied herself with the salad she had ordered for lunch.

"It's still early. Let's stop at that holiday bazaar," Hillary piped up when they walked out of the restaurant an hour later. Everyone hesitated. Marge wondered if they were in shock from Hillary speaking up or if they were waiting for word from on high. Not kind, she thought. If she spent too much time around Craig Carlson, she'd end up with a black-and-blue chin as well as a red nose.

"Why not?" Robert said. "We're not on the clock and the ladies can indulge in some shopping."

My son the chauvinist, Marge thought. She tensed when she noticed Craig's frown. But, as quickly as the frown had come, it disappeared and Craig treated Robert and Hillary to a condescending smile and a shrug. As if given permission to move, everyone headed for their car.

Marge hoped Robert wasn't aligning himself too obviously with Hillary against Craig.

Once inside the Civic Center, they fanned out. "Hey, Richard," Craig called out in a stage whisper that drew attention from every corner of the room, "isn't this your style?" He was holding up a filmy pink scarf.

Swiveling her head quickly, Marge saw Richard's red face and narrowed eyes. He took a breath and shrugged. "Nah," he said, "my girl likes blue."

Marge caught Richard's eye and was glad he noticed her smile of approval. Working for that man, Richard would need all the affirmation he could get.

After a few more minutes the men gathered in a corner to talk. The women scattered to check out the offerings on their own.

"Hillary, your purse."

Marge looked up to see Hillary accept a purse from Anne. Hillary looked inside it, probably to make sure all was in order, smiled, and thanked Anne.

"Are you sure it isn't Richard's?" Craig called.

Marge couldn't help herself. "What is your problem?" she asked.

"*Me*? I'm not the one with a problem," Craig said with his habitual smirk. Marge glared at him before deciding he wasn't worth her contempt. She returned to browsing. There would be no more smacks on the jaw for what she felt about that man.

A few minutes later, while holding up some Christmas tree decorations she was considering, Marge was startled to see a woman on the other side of the room with her almond-shaped eyes focused on Craig, as if willing him to notice her presence. It evidently worked, because Craig looked up. Anger sparked in his eyes and reddened his face. The woman stared back, her look reflecting smug satisfaction. With electricity charging the room, Marge glanced around at the others, noting that Ocean Shores had no lack of tall willowy women this weekend. This one was olive-skinned and Latin in appearance.

"I'm leaving," Craig announced. He marched out.

Hillary looked at the newcomer, and Marge's eyes followed. Marge didn't have time to decipher the expression in the almond eyes before she heard a commotion behind her. Robert had a hand on Hillary's arm, detaining her. "Let him go," he said. "If he wanted you with him he would have ordered you to come. Since Andrew also drove, we have room to get everyone home."

A chauvinist and a hero, thought Marge, looking around the room again. The apprehension she had been trying to ignore tightened the pit of her stomach.

Uneasily, they went back to shopping. Hillary purchased a scarf and mitten set she had been contemplating. They were sized for a young girl. "A gift for your niece?" Anne asked.

The pain and hesitation came and went so quickly on Hillary's face Marge wasn't sure she really saw them. Hillary's voice was barely audible when she answered. "Yes."

Marge shook her head. Underlying currents seemed to suffuse everything this afternoon. Must be too much wine in the middle of the day.

"Could I interest you in some boating or sightseeing?" Andrew asked when they had completed their purchases and headed out to the cars.

Marge hesitated, tempted. But—with a man this attractive after too much wine? "No, I feel the need to rest before I get back to my painting."

Andrew's look of disappointment mirrored what Marge felt, which was totally ridiculous. She couldn't be attracted to every single man who paid attention to her. First Charles, then David, then Kevin, and now Andrew? She needed to get a grip. Pete's face intruded, but she brushed it aside. There had never been anything but antagonism between her and the Bellevue detective.

The color of the ocean had changed to a deep aqua by the time Marge returned to her sketchpad. She put her watercolor pencils in a fanny pack on her waist, pulled on a sweatshirt and ear warmers, and climbed to the fourth floor. Framed between two condo units that jutted out beyond the end of the exterior hallway, the view of the ocean was narrow, but it was amazing how much more depth of beach she could see from this height. She shivered. The tunnel effect of the building on both sides of the hallway increased the intensity of the wind, already beginning to sharpen after the mild morning.

Leaning against the side of the condo, she propped her pad in the crook of her arm and began to draw. Her pencils would serve to sketch the scene in colors that could later be blended with a water brush. She would take a few photos to refer to for accurate color and shadow, and complete the work in the warmth of the condo with paint or pencils as needed to get the depth and variety of tones in the scene.

She had skipped the nap, but she hadn't lied to Andrew about her work. She wanted to complete one or two beach scenes good enough to add to her other paintings for the Christmas exhibit. As the artist in residence at the framing shop where she worked, the owner had given her permission to put on her own small exhibit in an attempt to increase her income. Of course, if the exhibits were successful and she sold paintings, he also took a cut of the profits in addition to enjoying the benefit of good advertising for his business.

When her fingers began to stiffen from the cold, she went back down to the third-floor condo and heated a cup of coffee in the microwave, wrapping her hands around it to soak up its warmth before taking a sip. The others had not returned from the different activities they had scattered to after lunch, otherwise she would have put off more work in order to spend time with them. Since they were still out, she could make use of the hour or so of good light she had left.

As soon as her hands felt warm and flexible again, Marge added a windbreaker and fingerless gloves to her outfit, gathered her sketchpad and pencils, and headed for the beach. She wanted to do some sketching at the jetty, with the water splashing up over the rocks.

At the top of the embankment she stopped and caught her breath. The ocean was constantly changing, each panorama more beautiful than the last. Now the waves, shimmering in the sun, crested and tumbled into a brilliant blue surface, energized by some force beyond her understanding.

After walking the quarter-mile to the jetty, Marge sat on a large log at a good angle and a bit removed from the boulders piled up in a ragged wall that jutted into the ocean, separating it from the quieter waters of Grays Harbor Bay. Waves, interrupted in their journey to the shore, hurled themselves into the rocks with a ferocity that sent water spewing high into the air. A couple sitting on a rock outcropping half-way up the jetty wall was surely getting showered by the water's return journey. As Marge drew out her camera, three young men scampered across what must have been very slippery rocks at the top of the jetty. Marge froze for a moment; she had to shake off the maternal urge to run and shout at them to come down before they broke their necks. As if they would listen. Taking a deep breath, she snapped a photo and sketched the scene without taking time to add the people. She would decide whether to do that later.

It was marginally warmer down on the beach. The sun, headed toward the horizon, added the warmth of its waning rays. Marge completed most of the sketch before clouds encroached from the east, dimming the sky overhead. She snapped a couple more photos before standing to trudge back to the condo. As she turned, she caught sight of Hillary's pink sweat suit. Hillary was jogging away from her and once again wore the hat rather than the headband. Her arms churned efficiently as she drew farther ahead. Marge frowned. Last night Hillary couldn't keep up with the group on the beach; this morning she shoved Craig and walked away at a good pace. At lunch she had looked like a rag doll. Now she seemed to have enough energy to jog. Was she bipolar or what?

Marge hurried her own steps. The kids must be returning to the condo by now and she did want to spend *some* time with them this weekend. She grinned when she recognized the echo of Ruthie's words this morning.

"Mom," Kate scolded when Marge walked in, "you're supposed to be on vacation. You can't spend all your time sketching. That's too much like work."

"When you love your work, it is a vacation to be able to

indulge in it," Marge said. "Besides, I needed to take advantage of the weather. It's not supposed to last."

"Well, hang it up for now and get ready to go out for the evening. We are joining Richard's gang at Galway's for drinks and music, probably moving on to the Home Port for dinner. Sure wish they'd build that casino they keep talking about. Nights would be a lot more fun."

Marge shuddered. That wasn't the kind of fun she looked for at the shore. Hiding her disappointment at not having an evening alone with the children, she grinned at Robert, who was sitting in the living room with his feet up on the coffee table. "Now who's making plans for everyone else?" she asked. "It's only a little after four. Do I have time to try and capture a sunset? If it doesn't cloud over too fast, of course. I may not get another chance."

Kate rolled her eyes. "Oh, yeah, take your time. If we're late, I'm sure they will start without us."

"Why don't you kids go in one car and I'll follow when I'm ready?" Marge asked.

"Because you might never show up," Kate said.

"No problem," said Robert. "If you're so anxious, Kate, you go on ahead and I'll make sure Mom stops drawing in time for me to bring her over later."

It took Kate more than half an hour to get ready to go out. Marge decided she might as well have accompanied her, since the clouds moved too fast, bringing with them a misty rain that effectively obliterated any sunset she might have painted. She was surprised, however, at the pains Kate took with her appearance. Was she trying to impress Richard? Could he be impressed by a woman?

Now she did slap her chin. No matter what Craig had hinted at so heavily while they were shopping, she didn't know anything about Richard. Nor was it any of her business . . . as long as he didn't hurt Kate. Besides, it was entirely possible Kate always spent a lot of time on her looks. Marge had little knowledge of how Kate behaved since she left for college and was free from parental control—a control that was often tenuous and difficult with the headstrong girl.

"Mom, I haven't had a chance to talk with you in a long time," Robert said after Kate finally left and Marge had finished as much as she could on her sketch. "How are you doing? How are your finances working out?"

Marge smiled to cover her irritation. Robert meant well, but he couldn't accept that she didn't need his help.

"I have a job I love," she said, "and my art classes. I've had to add a second class because my room is too small for more than four students. In fact, there is a space at the shop that I'm thinking of asking Joshua, the owner, if I can use to hold larger classes. I'm also beginning to sell a few pieces of my own. Nothing much, but it's a start."

"Mom, that job can't pay much more than minimum wage," Robert said. "'Are you telling me you can afford your rent and other expenses on that?"

Marge stifled a sigh. It was true she occasionally needed to dip into the money she had put aside when she sold the house. But last year she had begun to actively manage her IRA. And she was making small monthly contributions to her investment club account using the money she recovered from what Gene had lost before he died. All her investments had made steady progress through 1998 and 1999. Fortunately, she had not indulged in the dot.com mania, so this year's turbulence hadn't wiped her out and she knew that with patience, because she only invested in quality companies, all her stocks would regain their value and resume their growth. As she learned more about how to investigate the quality and prospects of a company, she should do even better.

In addition, she didn't intend to stop painting until she

could no longer hold a brush, but even if her income from painting never amounted to anything she would be all right. In fact, by living frugally now and investing regularly, she expected to be in good financial shape even without the widow's benefits on Gene's social security she would be entitled to start collecting in eleven years, at age sixty.

"I'm not telling you anything, because it is my business," Marge said. "I told you before, Robert, I don't need anyone to take care of me. I can manage my life." It would be nice if she could go to Robert for advice once in a while, but he was too eager to take over for her to risk it, and she would never be able to convince him that she was capable of handling her own finances.

It was six o'clock by the time she walked into Galway's with Robert and Ruthie. The group they joined didn't look all that animated for having started their drinking earlier.

"So, now that we're all here," Craig said with a look that seemed intended to make Marge feel guilty, but only succeeded in making her grit her teeth with annoyance, "what did everyone do today?"

For the sake of the others, Marge decided to ignore the implied criticism and do her part to try and loosen things up. "I spent the day sketching," she said.

"And, who was your model?" Craig asked, wiggling his eyebrows.

Marge's eyes narrowed. "Sketching beach scenes," she said.

"What a disappointment," Craig said. "And you, my lovely wife? Was your day as innocent?"

"Of course," Hillary said too quickly, her face reddening. "I wrapped up in a blanket and read by the pool; after that I took a nap."

Marge felt the tightening return in the pit of her stomach. Why was Hillary lying? Or being evasive? She had been jogging on the beach. Was she trying to hide a clandestine meeting—with Robert, maybe?

"We took a boat ride on the canals," Ruthie chimed in. "It was cold, but Robert let me use his jacket." She gazed at Robert as if this act of chivalry had earned her undying gratitude. Marge watched as Ruthie turned her gaze back to Craig, as if seeking his approval.

"Ah, young love," Craig muttered.

Despite Marge's worry about Robert and Ruthie, she felt a surge of relief. At least Robert hadn't been with Hillary.

"John and I read and took a nap," Anne offered, her eyes downcast.

"Uh-huh, those long afternoon naps," Craig interjected in a suggestive voice. Marge caught John's quick jerk, and Anne's restraining hand on his arm. Some kind of history there, she thought. It didn't look like it would take much for John to forget Anne had to be a team player.

"Kate and I investigated the island on mopeds," Richard said. "After that we drove out to the marina and toured the Nature Interpretive Center before hiking out Damon's Nature Preserve."

"How enterprising," Craig commented. He seemed about to say something else, stopped, raised his eyebrows with a knowing look at Marge, and faced Andrew. "And you?"

"A walk and a good book filled my afternoon," Andrew said. "And, since we're all recounting our day, what did you do with yours, Craig?"

Craig took a deep breath and smiled an enigmatic smile. "Oh, a little of this and a little of that," he said and ordered another round of drinks.

"Are you going to let him get away with that?" Kate demanded, looking at Andrew. From her tone of voice, Marge was sure Kate had seen the look Craig had thrown at Marge. "He starts it, but doesn't participate."

After giving Craig a considering look, Andrew shook his head. "I choose my battles carefully," he said.

Craig's mouth tightened. He glanced around the room, as if gauging the reactions of the others, before grinning complacently at Kate. "Take your best shot."

Kate shrugged. "I don't see how I could care less what you did with your day. But, I do believe in fair play."

"When everyone finishes this round we can head over to the Home Port," Andrew suggested, evidently agreeing with Marge that no more drinks were needed.

By the time they were seated at the restaurant, Marge found she had lost her appetite. She had had enough of this group from Point Brown and wanted nothing more than to enjoy tomorrow with her children. The conversation drifted over and around her until the meal was finished.

"I doubt there's much night life in this burg," Craig said. "Anyone up for a trip into Aberdeen to see what the big city has to offer?"

Oh, no, Marge thought, begging off and hoping Robert and Kate would do likewise. The drizzle would have made the switchbacks between here and Aberdeen slick by now. While Robert, as usual, hadn't had much to drink, the others had. Hillary seemed about to demur, but a look from Craig silenced her. A pained look appeared on her face. Andrew declined. Kate readily agreed to go, which surprised Marge, given her obvious dislike of Craig. However, the girl always did look for excitement. Once Kate agreed, Richard did, too. Then Anne and John fell into step with Craig. Marge was about to object to Kate going when Robert spoke up.

"If Kate is going I will, too, but I'll drive. Kate can go with me. That makes three of us. I can take one or two more." Ruthie lit up at Robert's words.

Marge was sure Richard was about to ask to join them when John unexpectedly spoke. "Anne and I will go with you," he said. Anne frowned and Richard shrugged.

It seemed to be settled until Craig objected. "That will put five people in Robert's car and only three in mine," he said. "Richard will go with Robert; Anne and John will ride with me."

Marge's automatic resistance to Craig's arrogance was swept away in her relief and gratitude to Robert. She didn't know if Robert had decided to look out for Kate or for Hillary, but the result was that Kate would have a safe ride home. Besides, he was a big boy, she reminded herself. If he wanted to get involved with Hillary's problems, Marge couldn't interfere any more than she allowed him to interfere in her life. Now all Marge had to worry about was what was developing between Kate and Richard. And if, whatever it was, it was shared by both of them.

Marge found herself outside the restaurant with Andrew when the rest of the party drove off in two cars.

"I saw on a flyer that there is a bit of Irish music going on back at the Galway tonight," Andrew said, standing close. "Could I interest you in a cup of coffee, now that the zoo has left?"

Marge felt herself stiffen against her body's response to his nearness. It would be nice to have a relaxing evening out with a pleasant companion, but she didn't know how to handle herself alone with an attractive man, especially one she barely knew, always wondering about his intentions. And, maybe more important, about her own intentions.

"No, I'm still tired from the drive and all the time I spent outside today. I think I want to go home and curl up in a warm bed."

Her face flushed at the mention of bed and she wondered how she would ever be able to trust herself not to give away her emotions. Andrew ducked his head and shrugged, but smiled as he escorted her to Kate's car. "Will I see you tomorrow?" he asked. "After that my group should be getting down to work most of the day and probably well into the evening."

"I plan on attending that small Methodist Church on Point Brown Road tomorrow morning. Would you like to join me?"

She was rewarded with a return of light to his eyes. "It's a deal. Shall I pick you up? What time is the service?"

"Ten-thirty, I believe. Anyway, if we're there by then we're pretty sure not to miss anything."

Marge spent a restless night, worries about the children keeping her unsettled. She must have dozed, because she didn't realize they had returned until she heard Robert's cell phone ring and his answer in a quiet voice. She glanced at the clock. Who would be calling him at three-thirty in the morning? Knowing the kids were safely back from Aberdeen, however, was enough to allow Marge to fall into a deep sleep.

She awoke to the music of the alarm at six-thirty Sunday morning, and found her movements unusually sluggish when she reached over to shut it off before it could disturb the kids. It had been many years since she had lost sleep waiting for them to come home.

She needn't have worried about the alarm awakening anyone. Robert was dead to the world on the Murphy bed in the living room. Feeling a little foolish, like an overprotective mother, she peeked into the other bedroom and saw Ruthie curled up in her bed. Kate's bed was empty.

THREE

MARGE WARNED HERSELF not to panic. Kate either got up early and made her bed immediately—highly unlikely—or spent the night somewhere else. That thought didn't help as she instantly visualized Kate spending the night with Richard. Or, worse yet, Craig. No, she wouldn't do that. She obviously couldn't stand the man. Anyway, wouldn't Robert have insisted she come home?

Throwing on her sweats, Marge shook Robert awake. "Where is Kate?" she asked. "She's not in her room."

Robert groaned. "Mom, she's a big girl now. I think she wanted to watch the sunrise or something." He immediately turned over and went back to sleep.

Marge glared at him. Watch the sunrise at three-thirty in the morning? What happened to being his sister's protector? She reached out to shake him again. Her hand was stopped in midair by an instant re-play of Marge, the mother of a teenage daughter, going into a complete panic more than once while Kate was in high school. Undoubtedly the anxiety tying Marge's stomach in knots was even more out of proportion to the situation now than it was then. After all, Kate had had her university and law school years, plus several years of living on her own, without her mother to obsess over where she was, with whom, and what she was doing. This didn't make it any easier to not worry.

The only thing that dissipated anxiety was action, so Marge set the coffee to drip while she gathered her art supplies. Kate would walk in any moment, she was sure, with a good explanation for her absence. Assuming Kate would think she needed to explain anything to her mother—which was not a given.

When the coffee was ready she poured a cup and balanced it in one hand, slung a bag with her art supplies over her shoulder, and climbed the stairs to the fourth floor. Instead of heading to the ocean view, she stayed on the east side of the building. She told herself it was because the wind was gentler on this side, blocked by the condos, and she could catch a sunrise. The idea that when her adult daughter Kate came home it would be via the parking lot on this side had nothing to do with it.

Looking far out into the distance, over houses and trees, Marge could see a sliver of light outlining the horizon. As she watched, the strip of sky changed from deep purples to a pink glow, giving a silver lining to the clouds above it. She spent some time trying to put the sunrise on paper, but worry about Kate's whereabouts interrupted her concentration, making her stop frequently and peer down at the parking lot. Sunrises don't wait for anxious mothers, so she repeatedly looked up to a different scene than that which she had left a moment before.

Marge was about to return to the condo when a car drove in. Kate jumped out, laughing and waving to whoever was driving. Marge almost tripped as she hurried down to the third floor to arrive at the condo before Kate.

"Kate, where have you been?" she cried. "I was so worried."

Kate didn't look at all chagrined. "We got home late and Anne wanted to talk so we decided to stay up and watch the sunrise, since neither of us ever gets up in the morning in time to do it. No one else wanted to join us, so we got some coffee at her place and went out to sit by the bay near the jetty. Sorry if you were worried."

With that she went into the bedroom, pulled off her clothes, and fell into bed.

Marge took a deep breath, released it slowly, and repeated it. Anger, followed by relief, dispelled the remnants of anxiety and she was able to concentrate on getting ready for the rest of her day.

Andrew arrived at ten fifteen. As warmly as Marge had to dress earlier, a sweater was all she needed now.

"The gang must have burnt the midnight oil," Andrew said. "No one is stirring at my place. How about yours?"

Marge grinned. "Not even Robert, and yesterday he was telling me he had turned into an early riser. Did you see Anne come in this morning?"

"No, though I did hear something while I was getting ready. How did you know she didn't come in until this morning?"

"Because Kate did. Evidently the two of them decided to stay up to watch the sunrise—at three-thirty this morning. They must have had quite a wait. I'm sure she added a few more gray hairs to the ones she caused when she was in high school. I'm glad she came in when she did or I don't think I could have gone to church."

Andrew studied Marge's hair. "Not a gray one in sight," he announced.

The church was a low, gray building fronted by a gravel drive and parking area. Folding chairs and recorded music highlighted the difference between this and the Bellevue church Marge usually attended.

"Are you ready?" The abrupt question from the pastor roused Marge from her reverie. After a puzzled moment, she decided he must be asking if they were ready for the kingdom of God. But it could pertain to being ready for whatever tomorrow might bring. She hadn't been ready when Gene died. Many young women today, she was happy to note, made sure they would never have to depend on someone else to take care of them. They were more ready to face the unexpected. She was glad that was true for Kate.

"What are you waiting for?" Now was never too late to start preparing, whether for the future kingdom or for the slings life threw at you.

As the pastor continued with his message, the differences in churches disappeared. This pastor, like her pastor in Bellevue, could plant questions in her heart that were sure to dog her for the rest of the week—whether they were the questions he intended or not. And this church, like the one at home, housed a community of people seeking God's direction for their lives.

After the service, Marge and Andrew succumbed to several requests to stay for coffee and get acquainted. Marge was surprised to discover that Melissa had listed and sold a house for one couple. Several other parishioners had retired here from jobs in Seattle and Bellevue. By the time they walked out to the car, Marge felt the rosy glow of good conversation and the potential of new friends.

"I don't know about you, but I didn't have breakfast this morning. Could I interest you in brunch?" Andrew asked.

Marge hesitated. She only had a short time left with the kids, but, considering how late they had come in last night, they were probably still in bed. Kate certainly would be. "As long as we're not too long," she finally said. "The kids have to go back this evening and I'd like to spend a little time with them today."

When Andrew dropped Marge off at Mariner Village after a delightful brunch at Miranda's, Robert and Ruthie were gone. It was no surprise Kate was still in bed. Marge wandered down to the office to see if the others had decided to play some pool in the game room, but no one was there, either.

"I knew I shouldn't have gone out," she muttered to herself as she returned to the condo. Changing into sweats, she wrote a note informing the kids she was taking a short walk on the beach and instructing them not to go anywhere until she returned. She slithered down the embankment into the usual sharp wind coming from the north. She started off in that direction, away from the jetty, in order to have the wind behind her on the return trip. Fifteen minutes later, feeling as if the brisk air had swept her mind as clean as the beach sand, she spotted Robert jogging toward her.

"I'm sorry I was out so long that I missed you this morning," she said when he stopped and leaned down, hands on knees, to catch his breath.

Robert shook his head. "It wasn't your fault," he said. "Hillary called to ask if we'd seen Craig. He left their condo soon after we returned from Aberdeen last night and never returned. We all scattered along the beach to see if he was out here."

Marge frowned. "That doesn't make sense," she said. "Where would he go at that time of night and still be out? Is there any chance he joined Kate and Anne to watch the sunrise?"

"No, he had no interest in going with them. But I suppose one of his lady friends could have followed him here and he went out to meet her."

"His what?" As soon as she said the words, Marge remembered the woman at the bazaar.

"It's no secret Craig has had numerous affairs—but I can't imagine even him coming down here with his crew and throwing some fling of his in their faces. He needs the group's concentration on work, so he can return to Bellevue with a team ready to perform. I'm sure you noticed the little confrontation at the bazaar, but it didn't look as if he was expecting *that* woman."

"I'd think he'd be more worried about throwing a fling in Hillary's face."

"Oh, he wouldn't worry about Hillary," Robert said, his voice bitter. "He enjoys throwing them in her face."

Marge glanced at him sharply, worried about his becoming involved in this marital situation. A warning was on the tip of her tongue when Robert stood and looked past her.

"Here come Hillary and Ruthie now," he said and trotted off to meet them.

Marge returned to the condo, unsettled by Robert's revelations. Rather than sit around and stew, she gathered her gear and went to perch on the edge of the embankment, this time to get the whole expanse on paper. It didn't go well. She finally decided she could only hope to capture little pieces, like the man and boy flying kites together. The scene made her smile. Her pencil flew across the paper as the boy's kite went down into the dunes. He clambered up the embankment after it, and was soon out of sight in the brush. In a few moments he appeared, standing on the edge of the embankment. He shouted and the man scrambled up to him. Had the kite been damaged?

She continued to work, trying to capture the windblown look of the boy on the edge of the cliff, when she heard sirens in the parking lot on the other side of the condo. She frowned, the pencil frozen over her sketchpad. Two men, one uniformed, the other with an unmistakable air of authority, hurried through the passageway from the parking area, around the swimming pool fence, across the path in the dune grass, and down the incline to the beach. The man Marge had seen earlier, flying his kite, was back on the beach, waving his hands to the newcomers, appearing to direct them.

FOUR

M ARGE RAN BACK TO the condo to deposit her painting supplies so the wind wouldn't blow them away. A peek in the girls' bedroom assured her Kate was safe. The sirens had evidently awakened Kate, since she was sitting on the side of the bed looking bleary-eyed and confused. "What is all the noise out there? Did someone drown?" she asked.

"I'm about to go back and find out. I didn't see anything like that while I was painting, though." It had to be something the little boy saw . . .

Ignoring the path, Marge returned to the embankment by the shortest route through the dune grass, plopped down, and slid through soft sand to the beach without benefit of the sloping path. Trying to brush and shake off the grainy coating the maneuver caused, she approached the scene of activity.

Two uniformed officers were cordoning off a large area

with yellow tape. A white jeep churned through the sand, stopping near the yellow tape. Marge edged over to get a closer look. Even though Washington beaches were public highways, this end of the peninsula was soft enough that it usually prohibited vehicle traffic. The jeep must have come from the last access road before the one at the jetty. That made sense, although it was a mile north, because the sand in the other direction, towards the jetty, was even softer. The jeep had an Ocean Shores Police Department insignia on the side.

Three men emerged. The plainclothesman Marge had seen earlier went to greet them and spent a few minutes talking with them before moving away with the jeep driver. The other two newcomers began inspecting the scene and directing a man with a camera.

Hillary stood stiff near the yellow tape, with Robert's protective arm around her. Ruthie hovered a short distance away, storm clouds darkening her hazel eyes and hardening her usually soft face. Andrew and the rest of the Point Brown Resort contingent were among the group gathered at the periphery. A police officer was talking to the man, evidently the father, who now held the sobbing boy in his arms.

Marge made her way over to Robert. "What happened?" she asked, her voice a hoarse whisper.

"From what I've been able to hear, it appears the boy was up on the dune rescuing his kite. When he looked down over the edge he saw a man lying in an awkward position behind that large piece of driftwood. He called his father, and his father called the police."

Looking to where he pointed, Marge gasped. It was the driftwood where only yesterday she had envisioned children playing. Unfortunately it had made a good hiding place for an entirely different sort of event. Poor kid. Obviously, the man was dead if the police were here and they hadn't rushed him off in the ambulance. Her own tears surfaced as she watched the boy crying in his father's arms; her arms yearned to reach out in comfort. No child could be ready for such a discovery—could anyone?

Marge eyes moved to Hillary and then to Robert. "Do they know who it is yet?"

Robert shook his head, but Marge noticed he also flicked a look at Hillary. Hillary's hand pressed against her mouth; her eyes wide and startled gazed past the scene in front of them as if she was in a trance.

The plainclothesman who had arrived first was standing back near the tape; his dark-blue eyes were concentrated on the activity but he was not taking part in it. What was that about? Marge edged closer to him. "What happened?" she repeated.

He brushed a lock of gray hair off his forehead; the familiar act suffused Marge with an unexpected rush of warmth at the reminder of Bellevue detective Pete Peterson, investigator of the two murders with which Marge had been involved. "Sorry, Ma'am, we can't say anything until we have more information."

"Have you asked if someone here can identify the body?" Marge persisted.

He narrowed his eyes and peered at her. Even though this detective was shorter and stouter, his bearing made Pete Peterson's image rise again. Suddenly he seemed to relax and shrugged. "Not my call. The beaches are public highways, which makes them county jurisdiction, and I'm Ocean Shores. Here to secure the scene. Now that they have arrived, I have no other involvement other than ferrying them in and out."

Momentarily distracted, Marge asked, "Ferry them in and out? Why?"

Now the detective grinned, a twinkle in the blue eyes,

nothing like Pete Peterson at all. "The county doesn't own four-wheel drive vehicles, even though it is responsible for the beach. Go figure."

Marge started to smile, but the scene in front of her wiped it from her face. "How did the boy know the . . . the person . . . was dead and not asleep or something?" she asked. She was sure he did know. Otherwise the effect on him wouldn't have been so devastating.

The detective glared at her, the twinkle gone. Marge's face flushed. Of course, she knew the police wouldn't divulge any information. Why had she made herself look like a nosy busybody by asking? She decided against pinching her nose under his close scrutiny.

Andrew emerged from the crowd and came to where Marge stood. "We should tell you that one of our party has been missing all day," he said.

The detective was instantly alert. "Name?"

"Craig Carlson."

The detective went over and talked to one of the men who had come in the jeep. Maybe the county detective? This one was tall and rangy, but still authoritative looking. When working on a case, all police detectives must have the same bearing—either that or she had Pete on the brain.

Why would she have Pete on the brain? She shook her head to clear the wayward thought and concentrate on the proceedings in front of her.

The man followed the Ocean Shores detective back to where Marge and Andrew stood. "I'm Lieutenant Morgan, Grays Harbor County Police," he said, his icy gray eyes all business. "This is Detective Barker from Ocean Shores. You said a Craig Carlson is missing?"

"Yes, sir," Andrew said. "He left his condo late last night— or rather very early this morning—and hasn't been seen since. We've been searching for him most of the afternoon."

"Evidently no one thought to look behind that log," Lieutenant Morgan said, his voice dry.

"No, sir, we didn't expect to find him hiding behind a log and we certainly didn't consider that he might be dead." Marge stifled a grin. Andrew gave as good as he got. "So, it is Craig?"

The steely eyes swept over the crowd that was gathered. "Who else here is in your group?"

Andrew narrowed his eyes and seemed to gather himself before answering. Evidently he had never dealt with the brick wall that protected police information. Marge thought the pause was probably noticeable to the lieutenant, too, before Andrew said, "That is Craig's wife, Hillary, over there." He turned and pointed to where the others stood. "Richard Wilson worked for him, and so did Anne Jacobs. That's Anne's husband, John, standing with her."

"And who is that standing with the wife?" asked the lieutenant.

"Robert Christensen, an old friend of Hillary's, who happened to be at Ocean Shores with his mother, Marge—this lady standing right here beside me." He grinned crookedly at Marge before looking around, but the humor didn't reach his eyes. "Robert's girlfriend, Ruthie, is over there, and his sister, Kate, there." Marge looked up to see that Kate had made her way down from the condo and was standing back by the embankment.

"And you are all staying where?"

"Our group is at the Point Brown Resort. Marge and her family are here, at Mariner Village."

"We'll need to bring the wife over to see if she can ID our guy."

Marge felt a churning of anxiety in her stomach.

"Can't I do that for her?" Andrew asked. "We were coworkers."

The lieutenant shook his head as he signaled a uniformed officer. "Better make it next of kin," he said. "And, if it is him, I'm going to need to talk to all of you as soon as I can wind things up here."

"My children both work tomorrow in Seattle," Marge said, watching as the officer went to Hillary and escorted her to the driftwood. "Is there any way you can finish with them first?"

Lieutenant Morgan stared a long while at Robert. "We'll see," he said, his voice noncommittal.

When the officer took Hillary to view the body, she made a choked sound. The officer nodded to Lieutenant Morgan.

"Do me a favor, Barker?" the lieutenant asked. "Get these two groups together somewhere and see that they don't do any more talking amongst themselves until I've had a chance to question them."

Detective Barker frowned slightly, as if reluctant to take orders from someone outside his jurisdiction. He nodded. "Sure, why not?"

Lieutenant Morgan raised his voice. "The show is over folks. Those of you who knew Craig Carlson, please accompany Detective Barker to . . ." He looked bewildered.

"The Mariner Village activity room," Barker provided.

". . . and don't talk amongst yourselves. The rest of you go with these other officers. They need to question you to find out whether you might have seen something this morning. Tell the officer where you're staying and how long you will be here. We will also need your home phone number and address in case questions arise later."

The small crowd was probably mostly visitors since rentals and time-share condominiums surrounded the area. They reluctantly turned away to follow the uniformed officers. What is it about tragedy that compels us to watch, Marge wondered.

Detective Barker ducked under the yellow tape and herded his charges up the embankment into the check-in and recreation rooms.

"You can play pool, watch TV, or anything else you like until Lieutenant Morgan is ready for you—but no talking," Barker said. "That includes you," he said, looking at Anne and John Jacobs. The couple, who had been huddled together as if to comfort each other, sprang apart like teenagers caught making out.

Tension filled the room. Andrew turned the TV on low and Marge was thankful for its diffusion of the oppressive silence. Detective Barker stood in the office doorway, occasionally speaking in a quiet voice to Jane, the office manager. Curiosity got the better of Marge. She walked over to Detective Barker. "So, after ferrying the county police in and out, you have nothing more to do with the case?"

He paused. "Well, we keep the scene secure. Other than that, as long as we're sure the murder happened on the beach, it's their ballgame and we take direction from them. If we find it occurred in the city and the body was moved, it's our case again."

"Complicated," Marge said. "But the nearest usable access is quite a ways up the beach and, as you said, it requires a four-wheel drive so it would be a little hard to move the body from the city to the beach." Though it might have been dragged or carried through the dunes and tossed over the side, she thought.

"Don't worry, we'll figure it out," Detective Barker said with a dismissive shrug.

"So, you're sure it was murder; not an accident?" Marge asked before he could turn away.

For a moment she thought he wasn't going to answer. When he did, it seemed to be with reluctance. "I guess you'll find out when the questioning begins, anyway," he said. "His body was at such an awkward angle the boy knew immediately that something was wrong. But we didn't know for sure he had been murdered until we turned him over and saw the hole in his chest. So, yes, he was murdered. And that's all I'm going to say about it to you."

Marge knew she had been truly dismissed and reluctantly turned away to stare out the window. Soon she saw a hearse drive into the parking lot; the attendants unloaded a gurney and headed down the pathway to the beach. It was twenty minutes later before they brought the gurney back with the wrapped body on it.

An hour had gone by before Lieutenant Morgan appeared, accompanied by a uniformed officer. Jane, her eyes like blue saucers, came out to the check-in counter to allow him to use her office for conducting interviews. Lieutenant Morgan surprised Marge by first talking to Kate, then Richard, then Robert. The minutes seemed to stretch interminably before Robert emerged. Ruthie, the Jacobs one at a time, and finally Andrew, took their turn trooping into the office like errant school children. Saving Hillary for last? Was he working by process of elimination? In which case, maybe Kate and Robert could leave tonight.

Lieutenant Morgan stepped out after Andrew. "You," he pointed to Kate, "can leave any time. Give your name and contact information to the officer before you go." He turned to Robert. "I'd like you to stay around while I complete the interviews in case I need to speak to you again."

Robert nodded, looking numb. He didn't appear ready to leave Hillary's side anyway.

The lieutenant beckoned to Marge next. Sitting on the edge of her chair, Marge felt like a misbehaving child sent to the principal's office. She had never been questioned like this before. The police had asked a few questions after she found her husband in the garage, dead from carbon monoxide fumes, but, since they assumed Gene had committed suicide, the questions had been quick and gentle. And Detective Pete Peterson just asked her to repeat, several times, what she had been doing and what she had seen when she found a body half buried in the woods a year later. Only after that murder had been solved, with her help, had Pete told her that, because she had discovered the body, she had automatically been a suspect. That's why he had asked her to go over the same testimony so many times.

Lieutenant Morgan's frown softened when he raised his head from his notes. "Relax, Mrs. Christensen," he said. "Your whereabouts have already been verified by Andrew Barnes and your son, who looked in on you when he got home. They also verify that you hardly knew the man or anyone else from that group. What I need from you is a timeline for and your recollection of every encounter you had with Craig Carlson's group here in Ocean Shores."

Marge did so, hesitating only slightly when she mentioned seeing Hillary exhibiting her varying degrees of energy.

"And Robert's friend, Ruthie, how well do you know her?"

Marge started with surprise. "Ruthie? Not at all. I met her for the first time when she arrived with Robert on Friday. I'm sure she didn't know the Carlsons either."

"What I'm wondering is, how reliable is what she tells us about your son?"

Marge stared at him. What did Ruthie tell the lieutenant about Robert? Surely she had given him an alibi. Her mind jumped back, sorting through everything that had happened last night and this morning, trying to place Robert out of harm's way. She frowned. Why would Robert need an alibi?

"Don't you find it slightly coincidental that your family happened to come to Ocean Shores the same time the Carlsons are here?"

Marge dropped her eyes so the lieutenant couldn't see corroboration in them.

"Especially since your son and Mrs. Carlson seem to have some kind of relationship?"

Now Marge looked up, alarmed. "Relationship? He knew her from years ago, when she was friendly with his ex-wife. That's all. They didn't have a *relationship*." Grasping at straws, she added, "Why would he bring another woman here if they were having a relationship?"

Lieutenant Morgan stood without responding. "Thank you, you gave a very thorough account. I will probably need to speak to everyone again to clarify a point or two after going over what I've heard today, to make sure I understand how it all fits together. In the meantime, you are free to go back to your condo. I understand you requested that your children be allowed to leave today."

"That's right. I'll be here until Friday," she said.

"As I said, your daughter can leave, and so can your son's girlfriend, though we may need to speak with her again. We'd like your son to stay around for now."

Stunned, Marge left the office. Lieutenant Morgan finally called Hillary in for her interrogation; Robert wouldn't budge until she emerged. Marge had thought that since Robert and Ruthie had come in together last night, he was only needed to corroborate the whereabouts of others. Lieutenant Morgan had strongly suggested they had more interest in Robert than that. She frowned. Exactly when had Craig been killed? If it happened in the morning, she could vouch for Robert until she left for church. But if it happened during the night, before Robert came in or after she left for church . . . A chill crept down Marge's back. How could Robert prove he had stayed in the condo? Marge had heard him on the phone when he came in, but once she knew he was safe, she had fallen so sound asleep Robert could easily have gone out and returned without Marge or even Ruthie knowing, since they didn't share a room.

Ruthie was huddled alone at one end of a loveseat glaring daggers at Robert. She didn't appear ready to go out of her way to give Robert an alibi even if she were able to do so.

FIVE

HE LIEUTENANT TOOK longer with Hillary than he had with any of the others. Robert paced the room, seemingly unaware of Ruthie, until she jumped up and ran out, headed toward the condo. Robert looked after her with a blank expression that told Marge he had no real feelings for her. Marge felt a twinge of pity for Ruthie, who must have built great expectations on being invited to the shore with Robert's family. How could Robert have used the poor, harmless thing that way?

Harmless? If she bore a grudge, she could do a lot of harm to Robert by lying about his whereabouts last night. And, how did any of them know Ruthie stayed in the condo last night? It could be Ruthie, rather than Robert, who snuck out to meet Craig. Was she naive enough to have been tempted by the attentions Craig paid her at lunch? Could she have been trying to get back at Robert for his attentions to Hillary, only to find she had to defend herself against Craig's unwelcome advances?

Marge shook her head. She was really stretching. Besides, Robert didn't drink much when he was driving, so he would probably have heard Ruthie leave, if she did. It was more likely that one of Craig's coworkers, all of whom seemed to have grudges against him, would do more than wish he were dead. What did it take to goad a normal person enough to make it happen? And how did it happen? A hole in his chest? Did that mean a gunshot wound? Or could it have been a knife?

Hillary finally emerged from the office, barely able to stay on her feet. Robert rushed to her side and supported her until Lieutenant Morgan came out to speak to them. He looked at Robert for a long time.

"I'll want to talk to you again tomorrow," he finally said, his voice hard. "You'd best make arrangements with your office." He looked around. "Be sure we know how to contact your lady friend, also. The rest of you . . ." He paused, narrowing his eyes as he looked at Hillary. "The rest of you can go back to your condos. But don't leave Ocean Shores without checking in with the police first."

"Can he do that?" Marge cried, swinging around to Detective Barker. "Can he keep Robert here on his say-so, without anything to arrest him on?"

Detective Barker looked distinctly uncomfortable, but Robert spoke up before he could respond. "It doesn't matter, Mom. I'm not going anywhere and leave Hillary alone in this mess."

The policemen left. Only Andrew and Hillary remained. Robert tried to pull Hillary into a comforting hug but she stiffened and pulled away.

Robert looked at Marge. "Mom, you have to help her. She couldn't have done this. You have to find the truth."

Marge stared at him. He was the one who had always told her to keep out of it and let the police handle things. He was the one who insisted the police knew what they were doing. Had her proving them wrong twice convinced Robert the police didn't always get it right?

Or was Robert somehow involved? He obviously cared about Hillary and resented the way Craig had treated her. Had something happened when they were out last night that tipped the balance?

No, no way. She found herself shaking her head. Robert was too smart to try and solve any problem with violence. He was also too smart to think he could talk Craig into treating Hillary better, putting himself in a position to lose his temper and strike out. Besides, if he was asking Marge to look into it, he must not be afraid of what she might find. "Please, Mom?"

Marge started. "I don't know what I can do," she said. "I don't know any of these people or the background that brought this about. I'll keep my eyes and ears open, but both you and Hillary will have to be completely honest with me . . . and with the police."

"Of course," Robert said as Hillary nodded tearfully.

Marge looked at the woman with narrowed eyes, realizing that if she were a police officer, she would attack while the suspect was weak to try and break her story, but Marge was afraid that if she questioned Hillary now she would completely fall apart.

"I'll have to talk to you tomorrow, to get as much background as I can on all the undercurrents evident in your life and your husband's work group. For now, get some sleep and try to pull yourself together."

"Thanks, Mom," Robert said as he led Hillary away.

Marge was startled when Andrew walked up to her. She thought he had left with the others from Point Brown. He turned to Marge. "I'm not sure I understand. Do you do investigations of some kind?"

"No," Marge said. "I had to find out what really happened to my husband when the police said he committed suicide. A year later my friend's husband was accused of a murder and I knew he wouldn't have done it, so I got involved. I guess I'm getting a bit of a reputation . . . at least for being nosy."

Andrew laughed, the sound jarring. "Well, I'll cooperate with you any way I can. And if you need help getting to any of my people, I can help with that, too."

"Thank you," Marge said, but she wasn't sure how much she wanted to rely on Andrew. She couldn't imagine him, with his cool and sarcastic wit, having anything to do with Craig's death—yet, what did she really know about him? He made no secret that he didn't like Craig and he had no reason to protect Robert.

Marge shook her head again. Robert didn't need protection. She was sure of it. She was!

She waved a weary goodbye to Jane and left the office. After parting with Andrew she headed up the stairs to the condo. Kate had waited for Marge to return to the condo before leaving for Seattle. "You going to solve another one, Mom?" she asked.

"I doubt it," Marge answered. "But I promised Robert I'd look out for Hillary's interests and make sure she doesn't get railroaded."

"I'm not sure Hillary is as helpless as she makes everyone believe, but I'll bet you do solve it for them." Kate gave Marge a big hug, slung her tote bag over her shoulder, and started out the door. She hesitated. "You don't think they suspect Robert, do you? That would be crazy."

Before Marge could answer, Ruthie emerged from the

bedroom with her overnight bag. "Kate, wait. May I bum a ride back with you?"

"Is Robert staying?" Kate asked, fear flashing in her eyes.

"I don't know and I don't care."

"Yes, the police asked him to stay," Marge said. She had to stifle a grin despite her anxiety when she noted that the soft compliant Ruthie had disappeared. The girl in front of her now was brassy, almost shrill.

"Will you take me or not?" she demanded.

"Well, sure," Kate said with a troubled look at Marge. "Come on; let's get a move on so we don't miss the ferry."

Marge rescued her art supplies from where she had tossed them. Had that only been hours ago? It felt like days. She checked her sketches quickly for damages before setting them aside. She was wondering whether to prepare some dinner for Robert when he charged in the door.

"Is Ruthie here? I've got to get her back to Bellevue. I'll try to get her on that ferry at Bremerton and give her taxi fare to get home from Seattle."

"Ruthie left a couple minutes ago with Kate," Marge said. "They're going to catch the same ferry." If she had expected Robert to look disappointed she would have been surprised. Instead, he seemed to relax with relief which didn't surprise her at all.

"Good," he said. "It would have been uncomfortable to take her anywhere after the way I ignored her this weekend. I didn't mean to, but Hillary needed someone and it seemed like I was it."

"Yes, you did ignore Ruthie. But you always were good at rescuing the wounded." She hoped rescuing the wounded was all it amounted to this time. "Is there anything else you can tell me about Hillary—or your relationship with her—or any of this?"

"No, you know everything I do."

Marge sighed. Somehow she doubted that was true. "You asked me to look into this, Robert. If you are being less than honest with me, it will make that job more difficult."

He looked hurt, but she remembered that puppy dog look from his boyhood, even when she knew he was guilty of whatever misdemeanor had been laid at his door.

"Do you want something to eat?"

Robert opted for a sandwich. Marge put together one for each of them while he paced around the room. When the sandwiches were ready, Marge discovered she had no appetite, so, while Robert ate, she stripped Ruthie and Kate's beds and took the sheets down to the office to exchange for clean ones.

"Anything new?" she asked Jane.

"From my husband the detective?"

Marge stared at her. "Detective Barker? I never connected you. But your last name . . ."

"Isn't Barker. I never changed it when we were married. Too many people knew me by my maiden name of Jeffreys. Anyway, to answer your question, I learned a long time ago that I don't listen and if I hear I don't talk about investigations."

Properly chastised, Marge returned to the condo. Robert wasn't there, which worried her. The more he made of his relationship with Hillary, the more the police would suspect him. Trying to calm herself, she made the beds, poured herself a glass of wine, pulled on a sweatshirt, and went outside to lean on the deck railing.

When she investigated the murders in Bellevue, she had known the people involved, which was why she could find clues the police appeared to have missed. Here she was totally in the dark. She didn't know the players, she didn't know the area, and she didn't know the police. Detective

Pete Peterson in Bellevue had never shared information with her that she didn't somehow pry out of him, and she was sure the Grays Harbor County police would be even more reluctant. Frowning, she wondered how much the county police would share with Detective Barker.

Marge knew that if she had any chance to keep her promise to Robert—and more importantly, clear Robert of any suspicion—she had to be more organized than she had been in her previous investigations. She had to make a plan and work the plan.

She stopped herself. When did it start feeling as if she had any business doing this kind of thing? Yet, it did feel right, almost as if it were a gift she had resurrected the way she had her painting after Gene died. She had to admit that as painful as it sometimes was, she enjoyed following the clues to find the truth about Gene's death and the murder of the man in the park.

But how did she keep getting involved in these investigations? Had she become a magnet for murder? She shuddered at the thought. As good as she might feel from ferreting out the truth, she didn't want to think of herself as an unlucky charm that made bad things happen. The ringing of the telephone made her hurry inside. What had Kate forgotten, she wondered.

It was Melissa. "It looks like I made a great sale, but instead of leaving tonight I'll have to stay here until tomorrow morning to get the paperwork started," Melissa said. "I can come after I finish that tomorrow, maybe even get there before noon."

"No problem," Marge said, but a wave of disappointment washed over her. She had been expecting Melissa later today and felt the need for her friend's support. "Uh, have you been listening to the local news?" she asked, shaking her head before the question was out of her mouth. Even if

Melissa had been listening to the news, no press had been evident today. It was probably too soon for word of the murder to have reached the outside world.

"Oh, oh. That sounds suspiciously like something happened and you are involved in it."

"I'm not really involved, at least not yet," Marge said. "But Robert has a friend whose husband was murdered here last night—or early this morning. The police have asked Robert to stay, and he has asked me to look out for his friend's interests."

"Is there reason to believe she did it?" Marge was relieved that Melissa didn't ask if there was a reason to believe Robert did it.

"Maybe. The victim evidently mistreated her, as well as everyone with whom he came in contact. Isn't the spouse always the first suspect?" After the person who discovered the body, she thought. But she doubted the police were going to consider that little boy as a suspect.

"You got me." Marge could hear the grin in Melissa's voice when she continued. "Looks like I'll get to watch the famous detective up close. Now I'm almost glad David couldn't get away. I wouldn't have been able to give him much attention while concentrating on what you're doing."

David Walters had befriended Marge when he bought Gene's BMW, giving her enough money to pad her income while she got her life in order. Through Marge, he had met and fallen in love with Melissa. The feeling was mutual and, after an initial stab of jealousy, Marge discovered she was happy for them both. She expected to hear about wedding plans any day now.

"Too bad you don't have Detective Pete Peterson to aggravate this time." The grin was still in Melissa's voice.

Marge stuck out her tongue at the receiver. She was glad this one was out of his jurisdiction, though. She hadn't had reason to irritate him in over a year and it would be nice if she could keep it that way.

"Have you met the policeman who's investigating it?" Melissa asked.

"He did question me, as well as Robert and Kate, and anyone else who could have any connection. But he's not the Ocean Shores detective, who I also met. It seems the beaches are public highways and, as such, come under county jurisdiction."

Melissa frowned. "Must be a bit awkward for the Ocean Shores guy."

"He did seem to resent it a bit when Lieutenant Morgan of the county police gave him orders, but he took it well enough. He's a laid back sort of guy."

"Isn't one policeman in your life enough?" Melissa asked, her voice dry.

Marge put her free hand on her hip and glared at the telephone. "Now, don't you start. I don't have any policemen, or any man, in my life and I plan to keep it that way. Besides, this one is married to the manager of Mariner Village."

"Really! So, did you get any painting done with all this going on?"

"Yes, before it happened. In fact, I was painting the happy scene of a young boy flying a kite with his father. Unfortunately the boy was the one who found the body."

"Poor kid. Are you sure you didn't catch anything meaningful?"

Marge shook her head. "Whatever happened occurred after I went to bed and before I started work on the beachside of the condo this afternoon." The question wasn't strange, though, since Marge's fingers often put something significant on paper that hadn't registered in her mind. What if she *had* painted on the beachside before church this morning? Would she have seen something or was it already too late?

Once they ended their conversation, Marge realized she was starving. It felt like forever since the brunch she'd had with Andrew, and dealing with the day's events had burned that up long ago. Retrieving the turkey and cheese sandwich from the refrigerator, she found a pen and note paper, and sat at the table. In case the worst happened and Hillary was arrested (well, the worst would be Robert getting arrested, but Marge refused to believe that could happen), Marge should talk to Hillary first thing tomorrow before the police put her out of reach. She'd ask Hillary about Craig's habits and his relationship with the people in his group. She wrote that down and took a bite of her sandwich. Next was probably talking to Andrew to verify what Hillary said plus add whatever else he knew from the workplace. He seemed to be the most observant and objective of them all. She wrote that down and took another bite. What next? On what pretext could she talk to the others, especially when that talking was to try and find out if one of them was the killer? On Andrew's say-so? He wasn't their boss even if he was a step above them on the corporate ladder.

Marge stared at the sheet of paper. That didn't look like much of a plan. She put her head in her hands. Why had she told Robert she would do this? What had given her the idea she had a talent for these things? "Lord, help me," she said. "Without that, I don't know what I'm going to do."

Marge slept late Monday, which dawned bright and sunny. Even the wind seemed to have died down. A carafe of fresh brewed coffee awaited her in the kitchen, with Robert's mug sitting in the sink. Instead of following Robert out to the beach, Marge started the day with a quiet breakfast to help gather her thoughts, many of which centered on how to get Robert to tell her exactly what he was doing here. After putting her dishes in the dishwasher, she called the Point Brown Resort and discovered only Andrew was home. The others had gone out to eat.

"We're not doing much cooking here at the condo," Andrew explained. "I don't eat breakfast, so I stayed. Why don't you come over, anyway? I have plenty of coffee, and we can have a good talk." When Marge agreed, he continued, "You'll see four different buildings at Point Brown. We're in the one called Atlantic Avenue, which happens to be the only one with three bedroom units. I'll meet you at the entry to the building."

The beach was so inviting Marge decided to walk it to Point Brown. Sunshine made the ocean sparkle, but the breeze was still cool enough to make Marge thankful it was at her back. She decided she would return to Mariner Village on the road, where it wasn't as strong. She wended her way up the path and to the front of the Point Brown Resort to find the Atlantic Avenue building.

"Three-bedroom condos are hard to find in Ocean Shores, and can be expensive. You have to buy five weeks a year at Point Brown," Andrew explained as he led her to the unit. "The company execs use this one for brainstorming sessions; for personal vacations; for achievement awards; and in this case, as a way for a new supervisor to work on team-building and planning. On this level," he added as they entered, "there is one bedroom and a bathroom. Richard and I are in this bedroom since it has twin beds."

They took a flight of stairs up to the next level. "This is the kitchen and living area, as you can see. The Jacobs' bedroom is on this level, too." He pointed to another flight of stairs going up. "And the Carlsons have the bedroom on the third level."

"Isn't it unusual for a supervisor to have only three people reporting to him?" Marge asked.

"Yes, it is, but this is a new team, with a new sales area. Craig would have hired two to four more people in the coming year, depending on the group's progress." He paused. "I take it you're here for information about Craig."

"Yes. I may not need it, if Hillary doesn't become a suspect, but I need to be prepared in case she does." She wouldn't even voice the possibility that Robert was a suspect. That would make it too much like real.

"There is no shortage of people with motives for wanting Craig out of the way. Whether they would go so far as to kill him is another thing altogether." Andrew poured two cups of coffee and led Marge to the sitting area.

"So," she said once they were seated, attempting to sound like an old hand at this stuff, "what were your motives for wanting Craig out of the way? You weren't affected by his promotion since you have an equivalent position already."

Andrew surveyed her over the rim of his cup as he took a sip of coffee. "You don't pull any punches, do you? No, although he was already campaigning to get the next promotion, which could be as soon as next year if our department vice president makes good on his hints that he's ready to retire. We would both be candidates for that position. It's a far stretch to think I would kill him now for something that might not even happen. Besides, I'm more qualified and he would only have been in his position for a year. Kind of soon to promote him again."

"So, all things being equal, you think you'd be a shoo-in for that promotion?"

"Well, yes, all things being equal." Andrew squirmed in his chair.

"But?" Marge prodded.

"All things being equal, Richard should have had Craig's position. Craig had a way of tilting things in his favor, whether by currying favor, spreading rumors, or whatever means it took to get what he wanted. I still wouldn't kill for something that hasn't happened, if I'd kill at all, but if you're going to get involved in this you need to have a clear picture of his nature."

"What about the others?"

"I feel like I'm telling tales out of school."

Marge was the one to squirm now. It did seem wrong, somehow, asking Andrew to talk about his coworkers. But, how else could she get to know this group well enough to figure out who killed Craig?

"It's all going to come out, anyway," she said, swallowing the guilty feeling. "And, by talking it through we will both be better prepared for whatever happens."

Andrew took a long drink from his mug, still studying Marge. "Okay," he said, "I'll tell you whatever I know about the others, but you have to talk to them, too, to get their take on anything I say."

"Fair enough."

"Richard, I already mentioned. He was in line for the promotion Craig got. In fact, he was more qualified for it so it was a surprise to everyone when it went to Craig. Craig let it slip to me one day, on purpose I think, that he had something on Richard and had threatened to tell the execs about it."

"Why would he do that? Tell you, I mean." Marge interrupted, frowning. Given Craig's behavior at the Civic Center, she had an idea what that "something" might be.

"Probably to intimidate me. To let me know he didn't intend to play fair in the future. Though I don't know what he thought he could get on me, I'm a pretty straight arrow. Anyway, I confronted Richard when we were well into the drinks one night and he admitted it. He said he had embellished his education and credentials somewhat when he was first hired. At first he refused to back away from trying for the promotion, figuring the background only mattered until he had proven he could do the job. In fact, he went to the execs and told them about it before Craig could. He evidently made a pretty good case for himself. He has worked for this company for over ten years and is a whiz at what he does, so the brass didn't fire him. Later, Richard withdrew from consideration for the Director position, probably hoping that would stop Craig from destroying his credibility with any group he might supervise in the future by spreading the story all over the firm. So his chances for promotion were pretty much nil as long as Craig was in the picture—or at least until he moved up the ladder a notch or two."

"Okay," Marge said, unable to hide her surprise. Not the motive she had been thinking of. "Maybe a motive, but a pretty weak one for murder. After all, he still has a job. What about that little byplay at the Civic Center?"

"I don't know where that came from. Probably something Craig thought up on the spot. I've seen no indication that Richard is gay, and I don't think it would cost him his job if he is. But if the motive we know about is weak, you have to admit mine is even weaker. Now, we come to Anne Jacobs."

Marge's head snapped up in surprise. Andrew grinned. "Oh, yes," he said. "As I said before, there's no shortage of people who have been hurt by Craig Carlson. Craig is . . . was . . . the office letch. No woman was safe around him. After an office party at which a little too much liquid refreshment had been imbibed, he got Anne alone and, to put it in old-fashioned terms, had his way with her. I don't know if it was closer to being consensual or closer to rape, but it happened. When this promotion thing came up, he threatened he would tell Anne's husband if she didn't support him. I guess Anne didn't think John would be able to deal with it, so she supported Craig. She may have realized she would be under his thumb as long as she stayed in the firm, and, if she took another job, Craig might be spiteful enough to tell John. That's the kind of guy he was."

"Is there any way John could have found out?" Marge asked. "And, how did you find out?" She also wondered when anyone in the company got any work done—they seemed to be busy taking "liquid refreshment" all the time.

Andrew studied the bottom of his coffee cup. "I don't know why Craig would have told John. He had Anne where he wanted her, and he wouldn't have if John knew. Unless Anne decided it would be better to tell John herself so she could get out from under. I think he had two reasons for telling me: one to intimidate me with his ability to twist people around and the other to boast about his prowess with women."

"But if John did find out, that would give him a motive, too. Especially if he thought Craig had raped Anne."

"True," said Andrew. "*If* he found out." He didn't sound convinced.

"Do you think Craig could have blackmailed Anne for more sexual favors?"

"I hadn't thought of that," Andrew said after a moment. "He doesn't tend to long-term affairs, but the sense of power might have tempted him."

Marge got up and began to pace. Anne made a good suspect, but she was presumably watching the sunset with Kate when the murder occurred. Did John not join them because he had other plans? How would John have lured Craig onto the beach late at night? "What is your group going to do now?" she asked.

Andrew had also risen. He was standing close to the window and staring out, oblivious of Marge's question.

"Andrew? What is it?" Marge asked walking over to join him. She couldn't see what had grabbed his attention.

"Oh, nothing. I expect I'll be getting a call from head-quarters soon. They'll use my cell phone, so I can be a tourist, I guess. And the same goes for the others. We'll be having no business meetings now, unless the brass calls and asks me to take over. But I think it would be useless. No one could concentrate. I wouldn't be surprised if they called us back to the office. The police will have to arrest someone to keep them here."

Marge pulled her sweatshirt on over her head and tried to tame the errant curls. "I need to talk to Hillary, too," she said. "Will you let me know when she returns?"

"Want me to drive you back to Mariner Village?" Andrew asked.

"No, thanks. Walking helps me think."

Robert's car wasn't in the parking lot when Marge returned to Mariner Village. Had it been gone before she went out? She hadn't looked for the car then. She had assumed Robert was out walking on the beach.

She hurried up to the condo; there was no sign of Robert nor any indication he had come back while Marge was gone. She tried to work on her paintings, but she couldn't concentrate. She sat staring out over the ocean, wondering whether Robert had met up with the Point Brown group—and Hillary Carlson—yet again.

She jumped when the phone rang.

"Mom?"

"Yes, Kate, what is it?" Marge's heart nearly stopped. When she could catch her breath, she started to gather her thoughts about Craig's murder in order to bounce them off of Kate.

"Aunt Diane was trying to reach you. She said for you to call her back when you got a chance."

Marge frowned. It took her a moment to shift gears from what was happening here. Why would Diane call Kate? Her sister should have her cell phone number. Or not. Marge sighed. Diane was five years her junior and lived in Northern Michigan. She had married a second time and still had young children at home. Known for being disorganized, she had probably lost the number. It was a miracle she remembered Kate's.

"She didn't tell you what it is about?"

"No, but she sounded distraught and said she had to talk with you right away. Do you think something has happened to Grandma?"

"Don't borrow trouble, Kate. I'll call her as soon as we hang up. This should be a good time because the kids are in school."

"Diane, what is it?" Marge asked when she reached her sister a few minutes later.

"I wanted to let you know Mom had a stroke. She will be out of the hospital soon, but I don't know how I can handle her at home. I can't take care of her now, along with raising my own family. You have to do something."

"What can I do?" Marge asked. "I can't afford to leave what little income I have and come back there. Alex is a good man and a good husband. He understands family responsibility. And Lisa is old enough to help."

Diane's laugh came out in a bark. "I should have known you wouldn't understand. You left home and never had another thought for the family you left behind. Lisa is already too busy with her own life to help me with the little ones as much as she should. You know teenagers. But mother is your responsibility, too, and you need to think about how you are going to do your share. I'll hold on as long as I can, but I'm not willing to risk losing another husband in order to keep her here. I'll put her in a home before that happens."

"Oh, I'm sure she would hate that," Marge said. "Mom has lived in that house since shortly after she and Dad were married. But, if that's what we have to do, how would we pay for it? Sell the house? Then where would you and Alex go?"

Guilt hovered over Marge when she hung up. Because she left home, Diane was the only one there to take responsibility for their mother. Of course, their mother had always doted on Diane, which was one of the reasons Marge moved so far away from Michigan to make a life for herself. And when Diane's first husband walked away, leaving her with an infant daughter, Mother had taken Diane back into her own home and baby-sat so Diane could get a job. Diane and her second husband, with their two young children, still lived in that house. Maybe Aunt Valerie, who summered in Traverse City, could advise her. Marge would call Aunt Valerie as soon as she had a chance to think things through. Although thinking things through would be hard to do right now.

The phone rang again.

"Marge," Andrew said, "the police arrived here shortly after the gang returned from breakfast, before I had a chance to call you. They took Hillary away for questioning."

"Was Robert with them?"

"No. Did you expect him to be?"

Marge took a deep breath. "He wasn't here when I returned so I wondered. Did it seem like they suspect Hillary?"

"Who knows? She had motive. I don't know if the police have anything more than that."

Marge felt a chill on the back of her neck. "Maybe. I had to let them know I saw Hillary in a place she claimed not to be," she said, her voice so tight it squeaked. "Did anyone else catch her in a lie?"

"I don't know any details, but I can't imagine that little mouse hurting anyone."

"I guess we need to start looking harder at the other motives. Assuming Hillary didn't do it, of course."

"If you don't believe her, why do you bother? She's nothing to you."

"She's a friend of Robert's," Marge said, biting back any further comment. If Hillary wouldn't kill to protect herself, would someone else—like Robert—kill to protect her? And, Hillary hadn't always been a "little mouse" according to Robert. Maybe when she'd had enough, her old nature asserted itself. "Do you think they're questioning Hillary at the Ocean Shores Police Department or at a Grays Harbor County location?"

"It was Lieutenant Morgan who took her away, but he didn't say where they were going," Andrew replied.

"Well, I think I'll head over to the library—which happens to be next door to the Ocean Shores Police Department," Marge said.

"Why don't we meet at the Shiloh Inn for lunch afterwards?" Andrew asked. "It has a nice view of the dunes. On a day like today I suspect we'll catch some acrobatic kite flying. You might as well have some fun on your vacation."

"If my friend hasn't arrived from Bellevue yet, we can do that."

But where was Robert?

Marge freshened up and headed to the police station. Hillary wasn't there. Detective Barker came out of his office to greet Marge. "What can I do for you?"

"What's going on with Hillary?" Marge asked. "It must be serious if they took her back to Aberdeen—is that where she is? Are they going to arrest her? Should her company be getting her an attorney?"

Detective Barker threw up his hands. "Whoa, hold on," he said. "I can't tell you anything about an investigation; I think you know that."

Marge peered at him. "How would I know that?"

"Because you've been involved in a couple." The glint in his eyes made Marge wonder what he knew and how he knew it. "Bellevue Detective Pete Peterson asked what you were up to now and guessed you might be a bit of a pest. Your connection with him isn't going to cut any ice with the Grays Harbor guys."

"You checked up on me!" Marge was dumfounded. "What possible motive for murdering Craig Carlson could I have?"

"Not me, them. They checked up on everyone, and your friendly neighborhood detective called me to find out what was going on."

"And you can talk to *him* about an ongoing investigation?"

Detective Barker shook his head and shot her a smile that said he didn't believe she was that dumb. "He's a policeman, remember? Different rules. Besides, I could only tell him what I know, and I'm not in on the investigation."

Marge felt a whisper of hope. Maybe she could find a back door to get some information. "What about the attorney?" she asked.

"That's up to Mrs. Carlson to decide."

"May I use a phone for a local call?"

Detective Barker nodded toward a phone. Marge looked at it and back at the detective. "Do you have a phone book?" she prodded.

He supplied one and she looked up the number for the Point Brown Resort. When she got Andrew on the line she told him what she had learned. "I don't know about you, but I think your company owes the wife of an employee an attorney. I'd at least have one primed and ready to go. And maybe the attorney can get Hillary back here if the police don't have anything substantial." Marge couldn't believe that the two little lies Hillary had told were enough to get her arrested for murder. Either they had something more or they would have to let her go soon.

"I agree," said Andrew. "Thanks for the heads up. I'll call and see what they want to do. Are you almost done there?"

"I guess," Marge said. "I don't know what else I can do."

"Let's meet at the Shiloh Inn and brainstorm."

"Sounds good, but let me see if I can contact Robert, first, and find out what time my friend expects to arrive," she said.

"By the way," Detective Barker said when Marge ended her call, "I don't know if the county guys will put any store in it, but Detective Peterson suggested you have a pretty good eye. He said we should get any pictures you drew or painted of the crime scene area or of the people involved."

"Most of the work I've done has been of that general area of the beach," Marge said. "Mariner Village is right above it, after all. But I wasn't painting on that side of the condo Sunday morning, so I don't know if I have anything helpful."

Detective Barker shrugged. "Well, Pete thought it might be worth a try," he said. "But who knows if the county guys would put any stock in a painting anyway. It's not my call, remember."

Something about his attitude told Marge he cared more than he said. If she cooperated with this detective, maybe she'd have a shot at getting more information.

His eyes squinted slightly, as if debating whether he should speak again. "I'm probably saying more than I should, but you might also consider lining up an attorney for your son."

Marge could only stare at him.

He shrugged again. "Just in case," he said, and turned away.

SIX

MARGE FOLLOWED THE hostess down the wide aisle between two rows of booths, each booth seating four. The outer row was against the windows and the inner one raised a step up, affording the best possible view of the dunes to each. Andrew, who was following Marge, nearly ran into her when she stopped short, wordlessly pointing at a booth occupied by Anne and John. They were both frowning and clutching their coffee cups tightly.

Marge stepped over to them. "Hi. I've been looking for you," she said.

Anne started and looked up. She seemed to struggle to put a smile on a face contorted with some emotion—what emotion Marge couldn't tell.

"I couldn't handle staying in the condo," Anne said. "Wondering if Hillary or . . ." she trailed off, glancing over her shoulder to where Andrew had stopped the hostess to notify her they had digressed.

"Why would Andrew murder Craig?" Marge asked quickly, guessing at what caused Anne's hesitation.

"They were after the same woman," Anne said in a whisper before Andrew arrived at the booth.

"May we join you?" he asked.

Marge would have smiled at him for so quickly understanding her intention if she hadn't been in shock. She ducked her head before Andrew could see her feelings written all over her face. She studied him beneath her lashes. He may not be Anne's boss, but he was in a position to make things difficult for her, so he probably thought he could count on her to be discreet. Marge would have to get Anne alone if she wanted to get more information from her.

"Yeah, I guess; sit down," Anne said with a notable lack of grace and a glance at John, whose dour face was anything but welcoming.

A waitress arrived at the table as soon as they were seated. Andrew and Marge checked the menu quickly while Anne and John ordered, and then gave their own order along with a request for coffee.

"You knew they took Hillary in for questioning?" Marge asked as soon as the waitress was gone.

"Yes, we were still at the condo when the police came," Anne said. "They found a gun in her room. They're probably trying to determine if it's the murder weapon."

Andrew's head jerked up. "I didn't see that," he said. "Did they have a search warrant?"

"You had gone to your room for something. When you came out they were ready to take her in. I don't know if they had a warrant. They only talked to Hillary."

"Do you know where they took her?" Marge asked.

John shrugged. "Aberdeen, I guess. Or Montesano; that's where the jail is. I don't know where they do their questioning."

"A gun in her room." Andrew was shaking his head. "It must have belonged to Craig. But, why would he bring it to the shore?"

If the police detained Hillary, Marge realized she would have no way to find out what Hillary had to say. No one else in the party was apt to know anything, unless one of them had brought the gun and put it in Hillary's room. If so, could that person have been Anne or John? Or Andrew? If someone was trying to frame Hillary, it was probably Craig's killer, and that person had to be one of the group in the condo to be able to plant the gun.

Marge frowned. If someone had come to the shore with a gun, especially one that belonged to Craig, the murder was planned ahead. Marge wished she could learn what they discovered when they traced the gun. She was sure Detective Barker wouldn't be that accommodating unless she gave him a good reason. And what good reason could she devise?

"Marge, are you with us?" Marge looked up to see Andrew grinning at her. "I'm beginning to get used to you disappearing like that every now and then," he said. "Anything you want to share?"

She shook her head. "I'm trying to figure out the gun angle. I presume Craig was shot; otherwise the police wouldn't have much interest in the gun." She thought about Detective Barker saying Craig had a hole in his chest. At the time she hadn't dared ask if they could tell what the weapon had been.

"You're probably right," Andrew said. He disappeared into thought himself. "But I suppose a gun could have been used to get him where someone wanted him and he was killed some other way."

"And the killer still took the trouble to plant the gun in Hillary's room even if it wasn't used to kill him?" Marge asked.

This was greeted with silence. Marge glanced up to see all three of them staring at her. "Well, assuming Hillary isn't the killer, of course," she said.

"Assuming that, yes," Anne said, sounding unconvinced.

"She couldn't have done it," Andrew repeated. "Hillary? Come on."

"Trust me," Anne said. "A woman can take only so much abuse, whether it is physical or mental. When that line is crossed, there is no telling what she is capable of doing. Craig, for whatever reason, treated Hillary like dirt but wouldn't let her go."

Marge's eyebrows went up. Anne felt strongly about this. Why?

As if reading her thoughts, Anne continued, "My oldest sister was in an abusive relationship. She took the kids and ran, but only because friends intervened and convinced her to escape before she could act on her desire to slit his throat while he was sleeping. She ran and had to keep on running to avoid his pursuit until he finally found some other poor woman to abuse and stopped stalking my sister. That woman wasn't so lucky. She ended up in prison for manslaughter."

And, Marge thought, Anne had evidently been sexually used, if not abused, and blackmailed by Craig. Could his demands have been for more than support in the office politics? Could they have reached the point where Anne couldn't take it any longer? But, again, Anne had been with Kate. She was the only one with an alibi Marge could be sure of. Glancing at the silent John, Marge could see no reaction to their conversation even though he looked grim as he studied the dune grass on the beach. She frowned. Was he truly that disinterested or was he feigning disinterest in order to deflect attention from himself?

"Oh, look, there's Carmella," Anne said. "What is she doing here?"

Marge felt Andrew jerk before he turned toward the entryway. Marge turned, too, and saw the woman who had been staring at Craig at the holiday bazaar. Her brow furrowed in puzzlement. What else was it about the woman that seemed familiar?

When she caught sight of them, Carmella turned and strode out of the restaurant.

"Who is Carmella?" Marge asked.

"Craig's latest mistress," Anne said, as she kicked Marge under the table and slid her eyes toward Andrew. Marge nearly gasped. Was Anne trying to tell her this was the woman Craig had stolen from Andrew? A look at Andrew's face told her it was probably true. If he had murdered Craig, he'd better hope he never got a close questioning by the police. He wasn't good enough at hiding his feelings. Was the reason he was so certain Hillary didn't kill Craig because he was the one who did it?

Marge couldn't believe Andrew would kill Craig, put the gun in Hillary's room, and proceed to insist Hillary couldn't have done it. Or, maybe that was a smart way to deflect suspicion from himself, thinking he wasn't endangering Hillary because the police wouldn't be able to find enough to charge her. She had to find out how Craig was killed and if the gun was the weapon. How was she going to do that?

"What's Carmella's last name?" she asked. Maybe if she primed the pump a bit, she could get some information out of it.

"LaCosta. Why?" Anne asked.

Marge shrugged. "Just wondered," she said, but the way Andrew was studying her told her he didn't believe it was that innocent.

Waving the waitress over and asking her for a box for the rest of her grilled salmon sandwich, Marge pulled out her charge card.

"Let me get that," Andrew said.

"No, I pay my own way," Marge insisted. "I'm going back to do some painting now. You stay and enjoy the view."

Andrew shook his head. "I'm finished." Looking at his plate, Marge realized he was. She and Anne had been doing most of the talking while the men ate their lunches.

Marge looked at him. "Actually, I would like to talk to you before I start on the paintings. We came in two cars, so will you meet me back at Mariner Village?"

When Andrew joined Marge at the Mariner Village parking lot, she cut through the pass way to the beachside of the condos and headed for the pool. The pool was covered, but the Plexiglas enclosure protected the tables and chairs inside from the wind, making it a pleasant place to sit outside, even warm when the sun was high.

"Now, I want to hear about Carmella," Marge said.

Andrew looked at her.

"I know you were interested in her, and Craig took her away from you."

"That Anne has a big mouth," he said. "When did she get a chance to tell you that?"

"When or who is not important. I know. So, what's the story?"

"There is no story." Andrew sighed and sat across the table from Marge. "I was dating Carmella and brought her to an office function. Craig took one look at her and set out to get her. It apparently wasn't too hard to do. Carmella left me without a backward glance."

"And you conveniently forgot about that when you were running down your possible motives for killing Craig?"

"Because it's history, and it's meaningless now," he said. "If Carmella was so easily taken in, she wasn't the woman for me. I certainly wouldn't kill for her."

Marge looked at him for a long time. She wanted to

believe him, and he seemed to be telling the truth. But he had reacted strongly when he saw Carmella in the restaurant. And people have killed for less.

"Okay," she said, "now I'm going to go upstairs and finish some paintings for the police. I'll see you later."

"Dinner?" he asked.

"Probably not. I'm expecting my friend this afternoon and since the police have asked Robert to stay around I want to visit with him."

"The more the merrier." He sounded hopeful.

"We'll see," Marge said as she led him out of the enclosure and went up to the condo.

She studied the sketch of the father and son flying their kite. She couldn't see anything suspicious, but she hadn't finished it yet. Maybe as she filled it in, something would come to her. She set out her watercolor pencils, water, paints, and brushes and went to work.

An hour later the painting was essentially complete. She studied it again. Nothing suspicious had emerged. Of course, the murder had already happened, so there may not have been anything by this time to catch.

On impulse, she put that sheet aside to dry and picked up the pencils. From memory, she drew the large driftwood log as she had first seen it while walking on Saturday morning. After finishing this with water brushes and paint, she studied it. Nothing; of course, it was too soon. Too late and too soon. It didn't look like her fingers were going to help her this time.

Grabbing the sketchpad and pencils, Marge went down to the beach. The log was no longer cordoned off, so the police had already finished searching the area. What did she hope to see? Still, she sat in the sand with her back to the ocean and sketched the scene again. The tides the night before had obliterated any signs of yesterday's activity. She couldn't see that the scene differed in any way from her Saturday painting of the driftwood.

Returning to the condo, Marge finished painting this sketch. She compared the two pictures to be sure she hadn't missed anything. She had managed to draw the log from almost exactly the same angle; nothing was notably different about the log or the sand around it. Only the dune grass above the log in the second painting seemed to be flatter, pressed down. Could the child have affected that much area when he was looking for his kite and discovered the body? Marge didn't think so. She had nothing to compare it to, since most people were careful to stay on the paths to protect the dunes. She imagined it would take something at least as heavy as a person—maybe a person being rolled over the embankment, to press down the reeds that much. It wasn't great as a bargaining chip, but it might help her when she talked to the detective. Or had the police already noticed it? Probably. They were professionals, after all.

Marge studied the two pictures again, followed by the one of the man and boy flying the kite. Despite the reason for her study of the last picture, she smiled. Without knowledge of the gruesome discovery that followed, this was a beautiful depiction of a father and son bonding on the beach. If nothing else, the exercise had given her one good painting for her Christmas exhibit.

She glanced at her watch. How late did Detective Barker work? She decided not to call and check for fear he'd tell her not to go to the station. She piled the paintings into the Honda and took off.

He was there. He studied her three paintings with interest.

"I'm afraid I didn't catch anything in these," she said. "Except for the flatness of the dune grass in the second painting. The crime scene people probably already noticed that."

Detective Barker studied it some more. "But you painted the first one from memory," he said. "It could be you forgot about the dune grass."

Marge shook her head. "I can't say it's impossible, but one of the things that amazes me is that my fingers don't forget what I've seen. I trust the one I painted from memory to be exactly as I saw it. Don't tell me the police didn't notice."

Detective Barker grinned at her. "I wouldn't know," he said. "I'm not in the loop, remember? But I'll see if I can find out."

"Another thing," Marge said. "There is a woman in town, a Carmella LaCosta. I'm told she was Craig Carlson's mistress. One he stole from Andrew Barnes, I understand."

The detective's eyes twinkled. "It does help to have someone on the inside," he said. "I'll pass the information along; it might earn me some in return."

"Like who owned the gun found in Hillary's room? And was Craig killed with a gun?"

Now the detective laughed aloud. "Pete did say you were a 'persistent pest.' Pardon me, but those were his exact words. All right, I can tell you Carlson was shot. I'm sure the news has that by now, anyway. I haven't heard about the ownership of the gun."

Marge made a face. "Wow," she said. "I've traded away all the information I have and only got half a loaf in return."

"You're lucky you got anything," Detective Barker said as he returned her paintings and ushered her out.

When Marge got back to Mariner Village, Melissa was in the condo, storing food in the refrigerator. Robert was not in.

"Between what I brought, what the kids bought, and what you brought, we are going to have to spend the rest of the week eating constantly," Marge said as they hugged in greeting.

Melissa laughed. Marge felt a rush of warmth. She felt so close to Melissa. They met when Marge had to sell her house, but it seemed as though they had known each other forever instead of only three years. Tall and lithe, with long blonde hair and light-blue eyes surrounded by small laugh lines, Melissa had become one of her best friends, a true confidante.

"I could hardly concentrate on finding a house for those people, I was so anxious to get here," Melissa said. "Have you been having fun?"

"It was nice spending time with Robert and Kate, but I didn't see much of them between socializing with the Point Brown group and the murder. The police asked Robert to stay, but I haven't seen him all day."

"How does Robert know the woman whose husband was killed?"

Marge explained Hillary's acquaintance with Robert's ex-wife, Caroline, how Robert had stayed in touch with Hillary, and how mysteriously they arrived at the shore on the same weekend. Her brow furrowed when she told Melissa how solicitous he had been of Hillary from the start. "And, I'm not sure she is what she appears to be. I'm sure I saw her two times away from the others, and she seemed different, much more energetic."

"Maybe she's one of those people who is at her best when she's alone," Melissa suggested.

"Maybe," Marge said, but the difference seemed to be more than that.

Melissa had driven straight from dropping off her clients at the airport, only stopping for groceries, so she grabbed a quick bite while Marge filled her in on everything that had happened. Before Melissa finished eating, Andrew called.

"The police brought Hillary back. Evidently they don't have enough to charge her, but they still seem to think she did it," he said. "They found no fingerprints on the gun, nor was there any residue on her hands that would indicate she had fired a gun. The police say she could have shot Craig and cleaned everything up afterwards, maybe wearing gloves and disposing of them."

"But that doesn't make any sense," Marge protested. "Why would Hillary clean her fingerprints off the gun only to hide it in her room?"

"Who knows how the police mind works?" Andrew asked.

Melissa answered a knock on the door as Marge was hanging up. Lieutenant Morgan walked in.

"I need to talk to your son," he said.

"Robert isn't here right now," Marge said.

"When do you expect him?" asked the lieutenant.

Marge felt her stomach muscles tighten. "I don't know."

The lieutenant's eyes narrowed as he peered at Marge. "I want to see your son at the Aberdeen police station first thing tomorrow morning. Be sure to give him the message." He strode out as Marge stared after him, feeling chilled.

Where *was* Robert?

SEVEN

"CELL PHONE?" MELISSA suggested, pulling Marge away from the door.

"Oh, of course." Marge breathed a sigh of relief at having something concrete she could do. The call, however, went unanswered. She left a message.

"He wouldn't answer the phone if he is driving," Marge said. "He'll check his messages when he stops, he always does. I can't wait for him. I need to get over to Point Brown and talk with Hillary in case the police decide to take her in for more questioning tomorrow."

"You're chattering, Marge. Slow down. Have a cup of tea or something before you go over. Do you think you should warn them that you are coming?"

Marge picked up the phone and was relieved to get Andrew's voice. "I think she'd better be up to seeing anyone who's trying to help her," he said in answer to her query. "Come on over."

Marge disconnected and turned to Melissa. "I hate to do this to you. We were so looking forward to spending some uninterrupted time together."

"I'd almost like to join you and watch you work," Melissa said. "But I'm more than ready for a soak in the hot tub and a nap. You go on and you can fill me in on what happened over dinner tonight."

Not sure how cold or wet it would be by the time she returned, Marge elected to drive the short distance to Point Brown Resort. Andrew let her in to what still seemed to be an empty condo. "No one wants to be sociable today," he said. "They're all in their rooms. I told Hillary you were coming so she would be prepared to talk. Shall I go in with you?"

"No. She'll be more apt to share with me if I'm alone, since I have no connection with any of you."

Marge climbed the stairs to the third-floor bedroom and knocked on the door. She could barely hear Hillary's faint "Come in." Opening the door to a dimly lit room, she found Hillary sitting on the edge of the bed holding a tissue to her eyes Marge saw a nearby chair and sat in silence for a moment, collecting her thoughts. She was sure a real investigator would be better prepared for an interview with a suspect—or victim—whichever Hillary might be.

"Why did you stay with him?"

Marge couldn't believe those were the first words out of her mouth. She put her hands up to apologize, but Hillary shook her head.

"No, don't apologize. That's a fair question, but it's one I can't answer. Not to the police and not to you."

"Why? What if it is the only thing that will keep you out of jail?"

"More likely it would help put me in jail. Anyway, I'd rather that happened than have it get out," Hillary said.

"So, whatever it was wasn't bad enough that you would kill to keep it a secret, but it was bad enough that you'd rather go to jail than have it get out?"

"I didn't say I wouldn't kill to keep it a secret. All I said was that I didn't do it."

Marge sighed. "Hillary, I promised Robert I'd look out for your interests, but I can't do anything without your cooperation. I asked Andrew to start working on getting you an attorney and it looks like that is all I can do." She stood and turned to leave the room.

"Wait," Hillary whispered.

Marge turned around.

"Are you sure Robert didn't really want you to stay close to me so he would know everything that happens?"

Marge froze. "Why would he want that?"

"Because he was determined to protect me from Craig. And that could mean he . . ." Hillary choked as tears welled up again.

"You can't honestly believe Robert would kill Craig to protect you," Marge managed through a clenched jaw. "Is this a ploy to keep from telling your secret?"

"No, I don't think Robert would deliberately hurt someone. But maybe by accident?"

"By accident? With a gun? Possibly with Craig's gun? Where would he get it? How would he put it back? Unless you're saying you talked him into it and helped him do it."

"No, no," Hillary wrung her hands and shuddered, then sat up straight. "If I tell you, will you still help me? And will you promise to keep it a secret? You have to promise. It has to stay between us."

Marge held up her hands to stop Hillary. She had to think a minute. She had never promised to keep a secret in circumstances where it could make such a difference. And even though she had sometimes been slow to tell the police all she knew, for fear they would stop her from investigating, she had never kept a secret from them. But once made, this promise could not be broken. Chewing on her lip, she threw up a quick prayer for wisdom. With no clearer answer, she had to trust her instincts. She sighed and nodded. "Okay, I promise." And I hope I don't regret it, she thought.

"The reason I left my previous job, the one before I worked with Caroline, was because I became pregnant. The father was not only married, he was an executive in the firm. When he found out I was pregnant he insisted I have an abortion and, when I refused, he made it clear I was finished at the company. I asked him if I quit voluntarily and had no further contact with him, could I get a decent reference for my next job. He agreed, so I resigned and went to live with my sister until my daughter was born. In fact, we both took an extended vacation so no one in her community would know what was going on."

Marge frowned. "Being single and pregnant is hardly an insurmountable problem in this day and age," she said. "How could Craig use that to make you stay with him?"

"I don't want my daughter to grow up with the stigma of having an unmarried mother," Hillary said. "When Caitlin was born, my sister legally adopted her and only the doctor, my brother-in-law, and I know the truth. My sister has been a wonderful mother. Caitlin thinks I am her aunt. Her life is happy and normal, and I'll do anything to keep it that way."

"And Craig found out how?"

"I made the mistake of telling Craig when I thought he loved me as much as I loved him. I thought love meant no secrets. When I began to realize what a monster he was, he said he'd make sure Caitlin knew I was her real mother if I left him or even disobeyed him. I couldn't risk it."

Marge's breath exploded in a small puff. "Hillary, if you

feel that strongly about it, you *do* have a motive for killing Craig. I can see why you don't want the police to know. But I think you're making a big mistake keeping it a secret from Caitlin. Chances are she'll find out when she's older; when she does, she'll feel betrayed."

Hillary was shaking her head. "She'll never know. I promised my sister and I vowed for Caitlin's sake that no one would ever tell her. I shouldn't have told you, but you wouldn't have helped me if I didn't. Now, I have to trust you to keep your promise."

Marge could see it was no use to try and talk Hillary out of keeping Caitlin's parentage a secret. She changed the subject. "Hillary, I saw you on the beach by yourself twice. You looked so energetic I could hardly believe it was you. Why did you lie about where you were when the police asked?"

"So you're the one who told that to the police. Marge, I swear to you, I haven't been on the beach except with Craig—and only when he insisted. Why do you think it was me?"

"I only saw you from the back, but I know your size and shape, and you were wearing that pink sweat suit."

"Mine can't be the only pink sweat suit on the beach. It had to be someone who looked like me. The police really need to check out Craig's relationship with Anne."

Marge stared at her. "Anne? Not Carmella LaCosta?"

Hillary managed a weak grin. "You've been asking questions, haven't you? Craig didn't bother to keep any of his other women a secret from me. He got a big laugh out of making Carmella think that once he got his promotion he was going to divorce me and marry her. But, he was ruining Anne's life, and enjoying it. She had to know it was only a matter of time before he told John about their affair."

"Affair?" Marge repeated. "You mean it went on after that once? And Craig told you about it?"

"Yes and yes. As I said, he loved to rub these things in my face. He must have seen some advantage in keeping his affair with Anne a secret from everyone else, though. Normally, it fed his ego for everyone to know how irresistible women found him."

"So, why do you think Carmella is here?"

Hillary stared at her.

"I saw her at the holiday bazaar and at the Shiloh Inn today," Marge said. Hillary had seen her at the bazaar, too, Marge thought, and looked as if she were expecting her. Since Hillary didn't admit it, Marge decided to keep her memory of that to herself for now. "Actually, I told the police about her, too; I believe they are going to question her. I wonder what she'll have to say for herself." Marge considered whether to ask her next question. She decided that being discreet would get her nowhere. "I'm sure you knew she dumped Andrew for Craig."

Hillary was still staring at Marge. Marge frowned. Was it possible Hillary didn't know? With apparent effort Hillary finally responded. "Yes. Craig was proud of the fact that he had taken her away from Andrew. But Andrew never seemed broken up about being dumped."

"Could he have been hiding his resentment?" Marge asked, still puzzled by Hillary's shock a moment before. What had caused that?

"Andrew? Maybe. But I doubt it. He's about the most upfront person I've ever known."

"Do you know anything about the gun the police found in your room?"

"It belonged to Craig, but I didn't know he brought it with him. I can hardly believe someone came into the room and got it, used it to kill Craig, then wiped it clean and returned it to the room."

"So, it was the murder weapon?"

Hillary nodded. "That's what the police told me. They believe the bullet that killed him came from that gun. I'm not sure they have proof yet, but they have no doubt." She shivered. "I never wanted that thing in the house, but, of course, that didn't make any difference to Craig."

Marge paused, anxiety snaking down her back. "Hillary, exactly what is your relationship with Robert?"

Hillary looked at her for a moment, her face softening. "When I didn't know where to turn and needed someone to talk with, Robert was there for me. I owe him my sanity. That's all."

Marge hoped, but wasn't quite able to believe, that really was all. She tried to think of what else she should ask Hillary but couldn't think of what it could be. When she left the bedroom, Hillary seemed calmer and ready to fall asleep.

Andrew looked up when Marge came down from Hillary's room, but she shook her head, smiled, and knocked on Anne and John's door.

"Could I talk with you alone?" she asked when Anne opened the door.

Anne seemed about to refuse. "I need to ask you about some things you might not want others to know," Marge said too quietly for John to hear. Anne glanced over her shoulder before nodding.

"I'll be back in a few minutes," she told John and closed the door behind her.

"It's a little cold on the deck. Do you want to go down to the parking lot?" Marge asked.

"I don't know what you have to do with any of this," Anne said as they walked down the stairs. "You don't know any of us. Why are you meddling?"

"Robert asked me to help Hillary and she has agreed to my help," Marge said. "Anyway, I think all anyone wants is to get to the truth. I know what Craig did to you," she added, almost grinning at her careful wording that kept the extent of her knowledge vague without lying.

Anne's eyes hardened when she stared at Marge. "So?"

"It gives you a motive for killing Craig."

"Oh, really!" Anne said, her voice filled with scorn. "I would have . . . in fact, I did a lot to keep John from finding out, but it wouldn't have been the end of the world if he had. Certainly not worth killing for. Especially now. Anyway, I was with Kate, remember?"

"Are you sure John didn't find out?" Marge asked. *Especially now?*

Anne stopped walking and turned to Marge. "Don't even go there," she said, a chilling glint in her eyes. "No way are you going to involve John in this." The steel abruptly dissolved, replaced by sadness. "I'm not sure he would even care anymore," she added softly.

Marge waited for some explanation, but Anne clamped her mouth shut and stared at her.

"I am not trying to involve anyone," Marge said. "I am trying to find out what happened."

"Do you know Craig was blackmailing Hillary to stay with him?"

"With what?" Marge asked, holding her breath. Had Craig told other people about Hillary's child? If so, how long would it remain a secret?

"I don't know. I guess if word got out it wouldn't have been effective any longer. Also, you should be checking out that Carmella. If Hillary didn't do it, she's the next best bet. Actually, she's probably a better bet."

"Because Craig broke up with her?" Marge's voice sounded as dubious as the felt about the likelihood of that scenario,

"She has that Latin temper. And she really thought Craig was going to leave Hillary and marry her. Craig told me Carmella had become too demanding and had to go. He actually seemed a little scared to confront her, and nothing frightened Craig."

It was Marge's turn to stare. "Craig seems to have told you a lot. Why?"

Anne looked down at her toes. "He knew I would stay on his team. Not because of what he held over my head, either. As long as he was rising in the company, I would, too. So he confided in me, partly to keep me close to him."

"Why would he need to do that? He already had something to hang over your head."

Shrugging, Anne seemed to consider her words before speaking. "He couldn't be sure what kind of a relationship John and I had. Maybe John would find out about Craig and accept what happened, or maybe our marriage would fall apart. If John were out of my life, for any reason, why would I care who knew?"

It still didn't add up. Especially not if Anne was having an affair with Craig. If that were true, why would Anne care what John knew or didn't know? Except for the possible divorce settlement if he found out. Marge shook her head. Without children, and with a good job, how bad could a divorce settlement be? She decided to keep her own knowledge about the affair quiet for now. With that, she couldn't think of anything more to ask Anne. Or Richard. Or Andrew. Saying goodbye to Anne, she headed back to Mariner Village.

Melissa was up and opening a bottle of wine when Marge arrived at the condo. "Any luck?" she asked.

Marge shook her head. "Everyone seems to have had a motive to kill Craig. He spawned a quagmire of lies and deceit in that company. I can hardly believe his superiors weren't aware of his maneuverings."

"Maybe they were. Maybe he had some hold over them, or maybe they saw something to gain by using him."

"Happy thought," Marge said. "How would you trust anything that came out of a company with such skewed ethics?" Marge accepted a glass of wine and sat in thought. "Hillary claims she wasn't on the beach the two times when I was sure I saw her. I can't figure out what that is about. She seems to be telling the truth."

"I know you have a good eye, but are you absolutely sure it was her?"

"If it wasn't her, who could it be?"

"Any number of women her size and shape might be on the beach this weekend." Melissa's face brightened. "I know. You need to draw what you saw. If there are any differences, your intelligent fingers will remember them."

Marge nodded. "I'll do that. Tomorrow. I've had enough today. Do you want to eat in or go out?"

"In," Melissa said. "We have enough food for an army, remember?"

When the phone rang, Melissa waved Marge to answer it. "You get that and I'll get dinner started."

"Mom, how is it going?" The strain in Robert's voice was unmistakable.

"I've learned a lot, but not enough to be able to make any guesses about who the murderer is," Marge said. "Where are you?"

Robert ignored the question. "How is Hillary holding up?"

"She may be stronger than you think. The police took her in for questioning today and may want to see her again. Craig was shot. The gun that was used was registered to him, and the police found it in their room, wiped free of prints. If that doesn't tell them someone is trying to frame Hillary, I don't know what it would take. Robert, the police asked you to stay in Ocean Shores. Where have you been?"

"I had to return to Seattle to reschedule some things and

put some things in order. I'm in Aberdeen now, just stopped at McDonalds for coffee."

"Well, Lieutenant Morgan wants to see you tomorrow morning. He wasn't happy you were gone when he stopped here today." Marge hesitated. "How important is Hillary to you, Robert?"

"You had to know her before she married Craig," Robert said. "She was so outgoing, energetic, in love with life. But there was always a little sadness to her, too." Which doesn't answer the question, Marge thought. She could only hope her rescuer son didn't rush into a relationship out of pity. Even if they did eventually end up in a relationship, they both needed time to find themselves first.

"Well, let's see what the police have to say to you tomorrow before we decide what our next steps will be."

Over dinner Melissa discussed her sale. "This was a big one," she said. "Even if the rest of the year is slow, I have a shot at salesperson of the year again. Can you stand another week at the shore next year? That's the reward for salesperson of the year in my company. I think it would be at Point Brown, though."

"As long as no one gets murdered next time! Are you sure you wouldn't rather bring David?"

Melissa grinned. "We'll see," she said. Something in the way she said it made Marge think those wedding bells might make an appearance before another year rolled around.

Andrew called shortly after they finished cleaning up the dinner dishes. "Could I treat you ladies to an after-dinner drink? I need to get out of the condo. It's too depressing."

"Not tonight, Andrew," Marge said. "Melissa and I are going to catch up with each other and hit the bed early."

Melissa eyed her when she hung up the phone. "Someone I should know about?" she asked.

"No, not really," Marge said. "Andrew is nice enough,

and he's certainly attractive, but I may still find out he is the one who shot Craig."

"Oh, good," Melissa said. "Well, not good that he might have shot Craig. Good that I don't have to warn Pete he has competition. Policemen seem to be more your type, anyway."

Marge threw a pillow from the sofa at her.

After a stroll around the protected side of the condo, they called it a night. But Marge didn't fall asleep until much later, when she heard Robert enter the condo.

Marge woke early on Tuesday morning. Sometime during the night she remembered the series of quick sketches she had done the first time she saw the energetic Hillary on the beach. Jumping out of bed, she went to find her sketchpad.

As late as Robert had arrived, she was surprised to see coffee ready and a used mug in the sink. She could only hope that this time he really was out for a jog on the beach.

Pulling the sketchpad out of her bag, Marge located the final two of the action sketches. She remembered Craig jogging past her and Hillary stopping him. Hillary seemed to argue with him, pushed at him. Marge frowned. From all accounts, Hillary wouldn't have argued with Craig; she was totally under his thumb.

Gathering her watercolor pencils and paints, she went into the living room and began to fill in the first sketch. The woman was obviously rigid and angry in her bearing, not at all compliant. She was Hillary's size and shape for sure, and wore a pink sweat suit. As Marge filled in the background, remembering the flock of seagulls pecking at the sand in the distance and the driftwood behind the woman's feet, other details began to come back to her. Hillary was wearing a headband the first time Marge saw her on the beach. This woman wore a hat. Either her hair was very short or it was tucked up into the hat. Of course, that didn't mean it wasn't Hillary. She could have started wearing a hat instead of the headband when she found out how chilly the wind was. But it did make identification more difficult. The distance and the angle of the woman's stance made it impossible for Marge to get a view of her face.

She went on to the last sketch of the woman striding away. In this back view, there was no way to tell who it was— all Marge knew for certain was that the woman was the same general size and shape of Hillary. But Marge had never seen Hillary move with the purpose this woman did, nor had she ever seen Hillary stand so straight. As Marge filled in the drawing, she remembered the woman had walked away with the pace and arm movement of a practiced speed walker.

Melissa came out of her bedroom, yawning. "How long have you been up?" she asked.

"I have no idea," Marge said, looking at the clock. "I was so busy getting at this while I was thinking about it that I didn't check the time."

"Whatever you're doing must have been compelling, since you didn't even drink that coffee I see beside you."

Marge looked down at the mug of cold coffee on the table. "You take a look at these sketches while I warm this up and get a cup for you," Marge said. "Of course, you haven't met the people involved, so I'm not sure if you can make anything out of them."

"Wow, your fingers not only have memory, they are as fast as a camera click. How early this morning did you start on these?"

"I didn't do it all just now. I remembered that I had started these sketches, so I pulled them out and I've been filling in the blanks this morning. The woman in the sketches is either not Hillary or it is Hillary and she is masterful at changing personalities when it suits her."

"You said there were two times you saw her. Do you have a sketch of the other time?"

"Not yet. That one I have to start from scratch, but the memory is quite clear. Let's see if my fingers can pick up any more discrepancies."

Marge managed a few sips of her re-warmed coffee before she flipped to a new page and began to draw. Before long she felt like she was back on the beach that evening. She remembered the stiff breeze, the slanting rays of a lowering sun. She noted again that this woman wore a hat, with no hair flying about. She stood straight and jogged efficiently, arms rotating close to her body, sand puffing up behind her feet. Her stride indicated strength and practice.

Marge shook her head. The size, the shape, and the pink sweat suit said it was Hillary. But the energy was wrong. She couldn't imagine Hillary having or being able to hide the athleticism the sketches showed.

The size and the shape were consistent but as Hillary said, anyone could have a pink sweat suit. Carmella, for instance. Take away her dark hair and intent face, and it could be her. Or Anne. Anne was close to Hillary's size, too. Just because she wore a blue sweat suit the first evening didn't mean it was the only color she owned.

Marge pulled the three sketches of the woman in pink out of the pad. As far as she knew, her testimony was the only thing that suggested Hillary was dishonest. Based on these sketches, she didn't think what she had seen was conclusive. It shouldn't be too hard to convince the police that it wasn't.

But, would it be enough to clear Hillary? Probably not, since they found the gun in her room. What was she going to do about the gun?

EIGHT

P OURING A FRESH MUG of coffee, Marge tried to think
of an avenue to pursue. The only person she hadn't
talked with was Richard. Oh, and John. John had
been at the table during the conversation at the Shiloh Inn,
but he hadn't taken part.

According to Andrew, Richard had accepted his fate with
relatively good grace. Still, as long as Craig was alive Richard
probably wouldn't try again for promotion. And Marge wasn't
as sure as Andrew that insinuating Richard was homosexual
wouldn't hurt his career. Even if he applied for a job outside
the company, Craig could get the word out about the falsi-
fied application and innuendo about his sexual preference.
Although, why would Craig care if Richard got another job?
That would mean less competition for him.

But Craig appeared to thrive on having power over
people, not only for what it could do for him but also for
the sense of superiority it gave him to "have something" on

them. No one, including Richard, knew what Craig would do if Richard applied for a position outside the company.

Marge had a hard time believing the mere supposition that Craig might do something would make it worth the risk of killing him. But, she didn't know Richard. Nor could she think of any good way to get him to open up to her.

She picked up the phone and dialed the Point Brown condo number. Andrew answered.

"Can you be absolutely certain Richard didn't leave the condo after he got in Saturday night?" she asked.

"Good morning to you, too," Andrew said. "No, I can't be absolutely certain of anything after I went to sleep. Why? Do you have some reason to think he did?"

"No, I'm practicing the art of narrowing things down by process of elimination. However, I'm afraid that doesn't eliminate him."

"I have some news for you," he said. "Someone seems to have tipped off the police about Carmella's connection with Craig. They picked her up for questioning as she was checking out of her room at the Canterbury Inn this morning. You wouldn't know anything about that, would you?"

Marge could hear the grin in his voice. That, more than anything he had said earlier, made her believe his claim that Carmella was history; not someone he would kill for.

"I am surprised none of you told the police, since you knew about her before I did," she said before saying a quick goodbye and hanging up before Andrew could make any suggestions to get together. She needed to be away from him to think clearly because, as much as she wanted to trust him, and as much as he seemed trustworthy, she still couldn't eliminate him as a suspect.

Picking up the phone again she dialed the Ocean Shores Police Department and got Detective Barker. "I have worked on three sketches of the woman in pink I saw on the beach.

It is impossible to identify her from what I saw which means my statement that I thought it was Hillary is worthless. Do you want me to bring them in?"

It took the detective a moment to answer. "That would probably be best. I can get them to the county guys if they want to see them. Are you sure you aren't putting what you want to see into the sketches?"

"I'm sure. My fingers don't forget what they see, and I don't try to change it." She paused. "Is there any way you can find out what the situation is with Carmella LaCosta?"

"I think you know better than that. If anyone is charged with the murder, it will become public knowledge."

Marge shook her head when she disconnected. "Life would never be so easy, would it? If someone else were accused of the murder, that would let Hillary off the hook, and if Hillary is off the hook, so is Robert and so am I."

Melissa laughed. "Don't give up yet. You have a knack for pulling bunnies out of hats, and I don't think you will be satisfied until you figure out who did it. But you can't do any more on an empty stomach. Eggs for breakfast, since I bought a half dozen and you already had some in the refrigerator. I'll whip up an omelet and toast. Anything else?"

"I think there is an orange or two in there. That should finish things off nicely. What can I do?"

"Not a thing. This is a one-woman job."

Marge picked up her sketchpad, sat near the good light streaming in from the deck, and began doodling. Before long she had six faces scattered over the page—the five remaining Point Brown residents and Carmella LaCosta. None looked so innocent that she would rule them out. In fact, she saw something hidden in all of them. She knew at least one thing Richard, Hillary, and Anne were hiding. Was Andrew hiding something about his relationship with Carmella, or something else? What was John hiding? And Carmella? Since she was apparently quite open about her relationship with Craig, what was she hiding?

To be fair, she had to add Robert's face. She was disconcerted to note how obvious it was that he was also hiding something. She had to admit he wasn't being open about his relationship with Hillary.

Marge pushed it all to the back of her mind when Melissa placed a delectable mushroom and cheese omelet on the table. "Ummm, not only an award-winning salesperson, but she can cook, too," Marge said.

"Thank you, ma'am. What do you want to do after breakfast?"

"First I want to take the sketches over to Detective Barker. After that, I think you deserve to do a little sightseeing." Marge frowned. Did she really want to leave the condo before she knew where Robert was? But that wasn't fair to Melissa, and Robert made it obvious he was in charge of his own life. There was nothing either of them could do for Robert while sitting around the condo. "Want to hike out to Damon's Point?"

"Sounds like a plan, but if you have any other leads you need to follow up on, don't hesitate to do it."

"That's the problem," Marge said. "I don't have an idea in my head. Maybe Hillary won't be arrested. Maybe the police won't zero in on Robert. Maybe I don't have to do anything at all. So, why am I spending my vacation worrying about it?"

"Because Robert asked you to? Or because you want to make sure Hillary isn't wrongly accused? Or because you're worried about Robert's involvement? Pick one."

Why had Robert asked her to? And when did Hillary become that important to him? Exactly how important was she? To what lengths would Robert go to protect her? Marge looked at her watch. And where, exactly, was Robert?

After they ate and cleaned up the kitchen, Marge carefully rolled and secured the sketches before following Melissa out the door and down the stairs to the parking lot.

"Let's take my car," Melissa said. She led the way to the other side of the lot.

From the doorway to the office, Marge heard a shout. "Look out!" Glancing behind her, she saw a car coming up fast. The car spurted forward at the same moment Marge grabbed Melissa and pulled her aside. They tumbled over and Marge landed on top of Melissa in a heap, feeling the heat and motion of the car as it sped by, followed by the sting of small stones striking her arms, legs, and face. Dust brought tears to her eyes when she looked up. A blue blur swerved onto the road, tires squealing and gravel spitting, and disappeared before she could bring it into focus.

"Are you all right?" Marge managed as she scrambled to her feet.

"The fall didn't hurt me. You on top of me, now, that's something else."

Marge's laugh was shaky. "You must be all right," she said.

Jane came running over to them, breathing hard. "That was on purpose," she cried, her face ashen. "The driver sat over there with the motor running until you came into the parking lot. I was coming out to see what he was doing out here so long, but before I could, the car suddenly lurched forward and sped right at you. He deliberately tried to run you down."

Marge steered Jane back to the office while Melissa limped behind them. "You look worse than either of us," Marge said. "You'd better sit down. I suppose we'd better call your husband."

"Yes, of course," Jane said, pulling herself together. While she made the call and they waited for the detective to arrive,

Marge and Melissa went to the ladies' room to clean out the dirt and stone from the scratches on their knees and arms as best as they could.

"So, your Detective Peterson was right. You do manage to get yourself in the middle of these things," Detective Barker's voice greeted them when they returned to the office.

"You got here fast," Marge said.

"I was on my way over, anyway. I have to go to Montesano and thought I'd take those sketches with me. What happened to you two?"

"Jane saw it better than either of us did. Someone evidently tried to run us—or me—down."

"Did you get the make of the car?"

"No, and not the license number, either. It happened too fast and the car was coming straight at us. All I know is that it was dark blue; probably a sedan."

"What about the hood decal?"

Marge squinted. "I can't remember if I saw it. I'll try to draw it later and see if something comes to me."

"The window? Did you get a look at the driver?"

"I don't think so. The area was in the shade, so I should have been able to see inside, but I don't think my eyes ever got that high. And with the dust in my eyes, I couldn't make out any detail."

"You?" he asked Melissa.

Melissa shook her head. "I didn't look back at all. The first I knew of it was when Marge threw me out of the way and landed on top of me, blocking my view."

"How about you, Jane?"

Jane was frowning. "You'd think I would have seen something, because I was coming out to see who was in the parking lot for so long with their motor running. I only had time to open the door before the car shot out of the parking slot so fast I couldn't even see if the driver was a man or a woman. Like Marge, all I remember is a dark-blue car, since I don't know one make or model from another. I'm sure Marge is right that it was a sedan. As soon as it started moving, I turned to warn them, so I didn't have a chance to look any closer."

Detective Barker gazed at them. "Now, you're positive everyone is all right? I think I should take you to the hospital to get checked out, or get the EMTs to come here."

"No need," said Melissa. "I'm sure I made a good cushion for Marge, and I'm only scratched and bruised, so no medical help is needed."

He continued to stare at them, not looking convinced. Finally, he shrugged. "I guess you'd know," he said. He frowned. "What do you think would cause someone to try, at the very least, to frighten you away?" He looked from Marge to Melissa. When neither of them had anything to say, he shook his head. "Nothing? That doesn't make any sense. Someone must think you know something. Anyway, I've called the lab boys to see if they can find anything of use. Jane, we'll have to block off the driveway for a while. Put out a sign for people to park along the road." He paused before asking, "Who do you know that owns a dark-blue sedan?"

Marge turned to stone. Her voice wouldn't work. Detective Barker looked at her sharply, but she still couldn't speak. Melissa's brow furrowed in question, then her eyes and mouth all opened into big circles.

"What?" the detective demanded.

"Robert," Melissa whispered. "But it couldn't have been him. He would never run down his mother. Besides, I think he's walking on the beach."

Marge beat the others out to the parking area and stopped short. Robert's car wasn't there. That knowledge barely had time to sink in before Detective Barker turned to her. "Now, what about those sketches?"

She looked at him blankly before Melissa ran to the other side of the parking lot to retrieve them. The sketches had flown out of harm's way when Marge let go of them to grab Melissa.

Back in the recreation room, the detective unrolled the tubes of paper on the counter top. "I see what you mean," he said. "With the hat on, and no good view of the face, no one could hazard a positive identification from these. I'll turn them over to the county anyway, for whatever use they can make of them. It does weaken their case against Mrs. Carlson, but only a little."

Absolute certainty that Robert would never do anything that would endanger her returned Marge's voice. "Doesn't this attempt to run us down weaken their case more? Hillary would have no reason to do that, since I'm trying to help her. It could only be someone trying to warn us away from investigating."

"A rather dumb thing to do, if that is the case," Detective Barker said. "Why do something that draws suspicion away from Mrs. Carlson?"

Marge couldn't think of a good reason, other than stupidity. Or possibly they wanted to scare her away, leaving no one to try and convince the police Hillary was innocent.

When the detective had gone, Melissa and Marge returned to the condo for warm baths and aspirin. "Are you sure you're still up to the walk at Damon's Point?" Marge asked when they were clean and clothed again.

"Yes, I think it's better to keep moving," Melissa said. "If we're going to get stiff, and we are, it should be after we've had our fun."

Marge laughed and opened the door, running headfirst into Robert.

"Robert, where have you been?" she cried.

"I was going to take Hillary out to breakfast, to give her a break, but she wasn't there," he said.

Marge frowned. "Andrew didn't say you had been there."

"He probably thought I'd be coming straight back here. I left my car in their parking lot and walked on the beach for a while."

"I thought you were supposed to see the police this morning."

"I called them earlier. They said they were busy with someone else this morning and would probably call me this afternoon. Why the third degree, Mom?"

"You'll be questioned about this, too, so you might as well be prepared," Melissa said. "An hour ago, someone in a blue sedan tried to run down your mother in the parking lot."

"What? Are you all right?" He paused; then looked stricken. "Wait a minute. You can't think I would do that?"

"No. Of course not," Marge almost shouted. But it didn't matter what she thought. What mattered was what the police thought. And in this tangled mess, what kind of alibi was Hillary for Robert, or he for her?

"I'm going over to talk to Detective Barker right now," Robert said, turning on his heel and racing out the door.

"Robert, wait! I think he's gone to Montesano," Marge called, but Robert was gone.

By now Marge wasn't at all sure she could relax and enjoy Damon's Point, but Melissa insisted. "You need a break," she said, guiding Marge back down to her car. "You might be surprised what will occur to you if you can stop worrying over it for a while."

"Do you think whoever that was in the blue sedan will try again?" Marge asked as she slid in and buckled up.

"I don't know," said Melissa. "If they were only trying to scare us, they probably feel they've accomplished their purpose. Even if they meant to run us down to put you out of commission, they may not pursue it for fear of being identified if they try again. But we can't rule out stupidity. No one said killers had to be smart. Are you nervous about it?"

"I guess. But we're prepared now, and we'll stay aware of everything going on around us. Do you think there will be other people at Damon's Point?"

"Hard to tell, at this time of year. We could turn back if you want."

"No. I hope I never let myself live in fear."

"That doesn't mean we should do something foolish," Melissa said.

Marge almost bit her tongue. She was often accused of doing foolish things to try to get to the truth. "Okay, let's think this through," she said. "There are two of us and as far as we know one killer. The police have the gun, and it is unlikely an amateur killer would have another one. With me so far?"

Melissa nodded.

"Damon's Point is flat. It's not a place anyone could easily sneak up on us. And we'll be past the area where cars are allowed. How am I doing?"

Melissa laughed. "You've convinced me. Let's go for it."

Damon's Point was, indeed, flat, as it is accreted land formed from sand deposited over thousands of years. The reed grass and brush, though, were taller than Marge remembered, providing ample protection for the birds that made this a migratory stopping place. As they drove up Marge realized the same reeds and brush could provide ample protection to anyone who did not want to be seen. But something about the clear and sunny day, with only a mild breeze on the spit of land sticking out into the bay, made Marge believe no one was stalking them. She was quite sure that if she had tried to run two women down this morning she would avoid them for the rest of the day.

She checked her backpack, which contained a sketch-book, water color pencils, water bottle, fingerless gloves, ear warmer headband, an extra sweater, and a couple of plastic grocery bags.

"Are we walking or working?" Melissa asked.

Marge laughed. "You know me too well," she said. "Let's walk out to the park by the cove at the end of the spit. Then, if you're willing, you can search for nice seashells for my art students and I can get in a few sketches."

"Deal," Melissa replied.

They walked the mile to Damon's Point Park on the end of the spit at a fast pace without talking.

"Coming to a place like this always makes me feel guilty," Marge said when they had reached the small cove. "This is a bird sanctuary, it is a specific type of geological formation, but when I come here I only enjoy the feeling of the place. I don't understand anything about it at all."

After a short rest, Marge gave Melissa a bag. It didn't take long for Melissa to gather more than enough complete seashells to satisfy Marge's students, since this beach had an abundance of them. The ambience was serene and beautiful, without the ocean's power and cresting waves, without kites dancing in the wind, and without the wind throwing water against the rocks of the jetty. Even though Marge didn't see much to add to her collection of drawings, she roughed out a couple scenes of boys searching for stones on the beach and skipping them across the cove, a calm inlet from the bay. It was a perfect spot for this activity. She also snapped a few pictures, thinking she could add something to them later.

Instead of returning to the parking area by the trail, Melissa and Marge cut across a thin strip of land that led out to Protection Island—the island was really an extension of the spit but the connection between the two was so narrow that it was called an island—and turned back toward the car, walking on the beach. They stopped for Marge to do a quick sketch of the marina on this side of the bay and of Westport, Oregon, on the other side. They stayed on the beach until they were near where the car was parked before finding a path that led back up to the trail and parking lot.

Melissa stopped and put a hand out. When she had Marge's attention, she pointed toward the parking lot. Another car was beside Melissa's car. It was the same color and size as the car that had tried to run them down this morning. Marge couldn't believe their assailant would follow them and park in so obvious a position, but there was no way to be sure. She pulled Melissa back to the beach. They continued past the parking lot and cut across scrubby grass and rocks to get to the marina. Signs told them the marina was closed for the winter and the restaurant that used to be there had shut down a few years before, but a short distance across the road they found a rental condo community.

They stopped in the office and consulted the phone book in order to call Detective Barker. He arrived fifteen minutes later and picked them up. When they returned to the parking area with the detective, a couple with two young children was returning to the car next to Melissa's.

"Well, I guess you now have us pegged as hysterical females," Marge said when the family had bundled into their car and driven off. "We didn't even get close enough to notice the two car seats in the back."

"Not at all," he assured them. "After your scare this morning I'm surprised you were brave enough to come out. And, I'd be very upset if you had crept close enough to notice what was in the backseat."

"We really didn't think whoever it was this morning

would try again, at least not so soon. But this car was too much like that one. I wish we had gotten a better look at the one that tried to run us down." Marge frowned. "I'll try drawing it this evening, but I don't think I ever saw it clearly enough to be able to dredge up any details. Did you find anything in the parking lot?"

"No. Do you think the car was the same make and model as this one? If so, that's more than we knew this morning."

Marge frowned. "Maybe. The only thing I'm sure of is that it was about the same size and color. When I draw it I may know better, but now I have to get the image of this car out of my head so I can trust my memory of the first one."

Detective Barker turned to leave. "I doubt you can be objective when you do that sketch. You'll be thinking about your son's car. Now, I'd feel better if you were a little more cautious. Stay where there are always people around until we get this thing wrapped up."

"Oh, sure," Marge said after he had left. "That would be a fun vacation, wouldn't it?"

"Much like what you said earlier," Melissa said. "I also prefer not to live in fear. This was a little bit of a scare, though. We definitely need to stay aware of everything around us."

Marge felt stricken and threw up a quick prayer for Melissa's safety. It seems she was always getting into situations that put other people in danger. They drove in thoughtful silence back to the ocean side of the peninsula.

"Shall we grab a late lunch before going home?" Melissa asked when they had reached Ocean Shores Boulevard. "I have a yen for some pizza at Dugan's."

"I don't know. What if Robert . . ."

Melissa gave her a long look. "You can't hold his hand, Marge. He hardly stays around long enough for you to do it, anyway."

Marge hesitated a moment, then sighed. "Okay, sounds

good to me. It's a shame we have to drive all the way back into town, though. Do you think anyone will ever build a restaurant down at this end of Ocean Shores?"

As soon as they walked into Dugan's, Marge spotted Richard, all by himself at a booth that would seat four.

"What luck," she said, approaching the booth. "Just the person I've been wanting to talk with. Do you mind if we join you?" This is getting to be a habit, she thought, barging in on people's meals.

"Sure," Richard said. "Glad to have the company."

"So, do you think you'll become the supervisor now that Craig is gone?" Marge asked after they were seated across from him.

Richard grinned. "You don't beat around the bush, do you? I like that directness about Kate, too." He sobered. "I don't know. Now that my history is out in the open, it's anybody's guess what the execs will do."

"But, you'd take it if it were offered?"

He shrugged and his eyes seemed to study something in the distance. Finally he looked back at Marge and shook his head. "No, I don't think so. I think it would be smarter to go for another job based on my experience in this one, and put no questionable claims on my application. In fact, I intend to start looking as soon as I get back to Bellevue."

Marge studied him. "That would avoid any guessing about your sexual preference. How long was Craig baiting you about that?"

Richard shook his head. "This was the first time, actually. I don't know where it came from, except that I haven't had a woman in my life for a while, and Craig was always looking for something to use to make others miserable. Of course, it wouldn't have taken long for it to get into the rumor mill, if that's what he wanted. And I'm not sure our execs would have a problem with it if it were true."

Marge frowned. "When did acceptance of homosexuality become the norm?" she asked.

"Since companies can get into a huge legal mess if they make an issue of it. Most would rather avoid it," Richard said. "But, as I told you, it isn't true. I hope you believe that, because I'd like to see more of Kate after this is cleared up."

Marge's frown deepened. Robert's fixation on Hillary was quite enough. She didn't need to also have to worry about Kate connecting with this dysfunctional group. She took a deep breath and looked at Richard, trying to decide what she could ask him. Richard let the silence go on for a moment, his blue eyes gleaming.

"No, to answer the question you don't know how to ask. I didn't kill him. I can't imagine killing anyone over a job, and my indiscretion was so long ago it wouldn't have a lasting effect on my career even if it were public knowledge. It could make things difficult for a while, especially if Craig used it to try to prevent my getting another job, but not difficult enough to kill over."

"Well, thanks for your openness. Can you tell me anything about the others that might help?"

He shook his head. "I think you know all the dirt, and I'm not about to spread any. I know you're trying to help Hillary, and I agree she is an unlikely murderer, but you have no official standing and I have no reason to believe anything I tell you will help clear up this mess. If I knew anything I would have told the police already. Now that we have that out of the way, let's enjoy our pizzas," he added as the server put their orders in front of them. "I meant it when I said I would like to see more of Kate. Do you think she'd be receptive?"

Marge managed a tight laugh. "You'd have to ask her. I know less about what she'd be receptive to than you do about your coworkers. She has a mind of her own."

"I gathered that already," Richard said, nodding. "Well,

I'll have to stick out my neck and see what happens. It won't be the first time I've done that; let's hope I don't get it chopped at this time."

Was it because Richard was so much older than Kate that Marge hoped nothing would come of his intentions? Because, except for that, she found herself liking this man.

"Have you never married?" she asked.

"Married too young; divorced within a few years. Once burned, though, I've been reluctant to put myself in that position again."

"Did you know Carmella LaCosta at all?"

"Some. She was around often, first with Andrew and then with Craig."

Marge looked up, startled.

"Craig never bothered to hide his other women. He even invited them to functions when Hillary would be there."

"How did Carmella act when Hillary was present?"

"She ignored Hillary, put on a queen-of-the-ball attitude, and acted possessive with Craig. As if Hillary would care. She probably would have been relieved if Craig had left her."

"How could the executives in your company promote such a blatantly amoral person?"

Richard's brows drew together again. Marge thought that if he kept that up, in a few years he'd have the studied look of a stodgy professor. "I've often wondered. My guess is that he put as much effort into digging up dirt on them as he did the rest of us. They probably had no choice."

Very possible, Marge thought. At this point, she wasn't in the least bit surprised that Craig Carlson got himself murdered. The only surprise was that it hadn't happened sooner.

Did that mean the motive for the murder was something Craig had done recently? How long had Robert been seeing Hillary?

NINE

‿‿

DRAWING WHAT MARGE remembered of the car that afternoon did nothing to narrow down the make and model, although it verified that the size was similar to the car they had seen at Damon's Point and the color was dark blue. As she suspected, her view of the one in the parking lot had been too close, too fleeting, and too blurred for her to take in the exact shape or any other details. It was, however, enough to rule out any cars that weren't dark-blue sedans. Craig's car was a red convertible, so that probably ruled out Hillary. Robert's was dark blue, but it was beyond belief that he would have run down his mother in the parking lot.

"I'm about to give up," Marge said. "I don't know what made me think I could solve this, anyway."

"Maybe because you've done it before." Melissa paused, frowning. "I keep thinking about the fact that Craig probably had the executives of that company over the barrel. And they are the ones who sent him here. What would prevent one of them from driving to Ocean Shores, luring him to the beach, killing him, and driving back to Bellevue without anyone knowing they were here?"

"Nothing. But why would they come back to run us down and put their car in public view? That doesn't make sense."

"See?" Melissa said. "You cut right to the chase. Don't give up. Keep listening and putting your logical mind to work." She frowned. "So, they didn't drive back home. They stayed over, maybe with an assumed name and a rental car."

Marge shook her head. "It would make even less sense for them to call attention to themselves by threatening us than it would for one of the group at Point Brown. If no one knew they were here, what could they fear from me?"

Of course, murder doesn't make sense, and the person who commits murder isn't thinking straight. Marge found out how skewed a person's thinking could be the last time she was involved with a homicide. If Craig's murderer used an assumed name, and maybe a rental car, would he or she still be here? How would she find out? Even if she could send the entire Point Brown group to all the motels in the area, what were the chances they would run into this person?

The phone rang. Marge picked it up.

"I'm beginning to feel like you are avoiding me," Andrew said. "May I take you and your friend out to dinner tonight?"

"I'm not sure what we're doing. Would you like to come over for a glass of wine while we discuss it? We wouldn't want you to feel neglected."

"Sounds like a plan, but do you mind if I bring my own beverage? I'm more of a beer drinker."

"No, don't do that. Kate didn't take her leftover beer with

her, and Robert doesn't drink that much. You can do us a favor and drink some of it."

Hanging up, Marge told herself that she didn't want to alienate Andrew, because he was her best source of information about that group. That was why she asked him over. But, she couldn't hide the smile that emerged at the prospect of seeing him; not even when she caught Melissa giving her a sidelong glance.

"Do you think Richard will be offered Craig's position now?" Marge asked Andrew when they were settled with their drinks.

Andrew paused a moment, his green eyes dark with thought. "If they truly accept that his job performance over the years outweighs his dishonesty on the application, maybe. But if it were up to me, I'm not sure I would promote him. If another situation came up where he could get ahead if he were dishonest, would he do it? I think our execs would keep his lies quiet if he went out to get another job, and in his place that's what I'd do."

"Especially if Craig already started rumors about Richard's sexual preference," Marge said.

"That's hard to know. Our executives are a bit older, so they might have difficulty with that, even though they could run into legal trouble if there were any hint they let Richard go because of it and he contested it. He might run into some flak in the office, though. Not everyone is comfortable around gays, and some people get outright nasty."

Melissa frowned. "I wonder if we'll ever reach the point when we can let people live their own lives."

"Probably not," Marge said. "Ever since Adam and Eve ate of the tree of knowledge of good and evil, people have thought they could decide who was good and who was evil. Why do you think God forbade it?"

"Does that mean you think homosexuality is an acceptable life choice?" Andrew asked.

"I didn't say that. Quite frankly, I have no idea and find discussion of it very confusing. But fortunately, it's not up to me to decide for other people. It's between them and God.

"So, to get back to our problem," Marge continued, "if Richard doesn't get the position, who does?"

"That only leaves Anne, who would have to start a whole new sales team. Or the execs might rethink that idea and add to my group instead."

Marge narrowed her eyes slightly and peered at Andrew. "So, you might have something to gain from Craig's death after all."

Andrew laughed. "Yeah, more work," he said. "It wouldn't change my position, but it would increase the number of people I supervise."

"But Anne still has enough experience to challenge you for the next promotion?"

Now Andrew was shaking his head. "You keep trying to make this about work. What kind of person would murder someone to get his position? It doesn't make sense to me."

Melissa piped in, "As Marge often says, murder doesn't make sense."

"How is Hillary holding up?" Marge asked, deciding it was time to change the subject.

"She's doing fine. She can't really mourn Craig's death—we all know what kind of a marriage that was. She's over the shock of it now, so her only worry is being accused of killing him."

"I can't get a handle on this," Marge said. "I hope the police are doing better than I am, and not spending all their time building a case against Hillary." Or Robert, she thought. "Andrew, is there someone at the office you could call who would know if anyone other than your group has been away for the last two or three days?"

Andrew shook his head again as he gazed at her. "Now you really are stretching. If you can't make it someone here, you try to make it someone else from the office. I think passion is more likely to be a motive than job promotion. I'd think you'd be concentrating on Carmella LaCosta."

"You think Carmella cared that much for Craig?"

Andrew laughed. "No, I doubt Carmella is capable of that kind of passion. She had a passion to get ahead, to better herself. She hung her hopes on me until she met Craig. He looked like more of a winner, so she dumped me and bet on getting Craig to divorce Hillary and marry her. When her plans were thwarted, she could have been angry enough to kill him. That kind of malice leaves more room for planning a murder than love, for which one would tend to lash out in the spur of the moment. This murder appears to have been planned, down to returning the gun to Hillary's room."

Marge gazed at him. "That makes a lot of sense. Where did I get the idea Carmella was the passionate type with a, excuse me for the stereotype, Latin temper?" She frowned in thought, but it didn't come to her. "I wonder how she knew where to find Craig? He didn't seem happy to see her at the bazaar. Would he have told her where he was if he didn't want her to come?" She paused again. "Maybe someone else told her. Someone who wanted her here to make trouble for Craig. Or someone who wanted to use her to distract the police. I wonder if they are still holding her or if she has already left town."

Marge picked up the phone to call the police station, only to be told Detective Barker was off duty until tomorrow morning.

"She was at the Canterbury Inn. I don't think she'll still

be registered because she had checked out when the police picked her up this morning. Would you recognize her car, Andrew?"

"Yes, she drives a blue Dodge sedan."

Marge cocked her head, exchanging a look with Melissa. Why hadn't anyone known Carmella drove a blue sedan? "Is that invitation to dinner still good?"

"Of course. What did you have in mind?"

"First we'll stop downstairs and see if Jane is at the desk and, if so, if she'll get in touch with her husband for us. Maybe he knows whether Carmella is still with the police or, if not, when they let her go. If she is still in custody or was released a short time ago, we'll go to the Canterbury Inn parking lot and see if her car is still there. If not, we give up and go to Mariah's for dinner. It's right next door at the Polynesian."

"That's a lot of ifs, but we end up at the right place, so let's go for it."

"Guys," Melissa broke in. "I hate to be a party pooper, but Marge landed on me pretty hard this morning and I'm feeling stiff and sore. You go ahead. I'll be happier with another warm bath and bed."

"Are you sure?" Marge asked, contrite. "Now I feel bad leaving you again."

"Don't," Melissa said. "I'm doing what I want to do, and you're doing what you need to do. No harm, no foul."

"Excuse me," Andrew said as he and Marge headed to the condo office. "You landed on top of Melissa? How did that happen?"

Marge shook her head. Of course Andrew didn't know. "Someone in a blue sedan tried to run down us—or me—in the parking lot this morning."

"What?" Andrew interrupted. "Are you sure you're okay?"

"I'm fine," Marge said with a laugh. "I landed on top of Melissa, remember?"

"And Carmella drives a blue sedan," Andrew said.

"And Carmella was being interviewed by the police when we were run down," Marge added.

They entered the condo office. Marge was relieved to see Jane was still on duty. "Don't you ever take any time off?" she asked.

Jane laughed. "I'll be leaving soon. I like to make sure most of our newly arrived guests are checked in before I leave."

"Do you get many in the middle of the week?"

"A few. Especially during the off season. They can make a last-minute reservation and pay a nominal fee instead of using their annual credits. Today we had three check in."

"Jane, would it be possible for you to get in touch with Detective Barker so we can ask him a question? I know he's off duty, but I have one question I need answered right now, if he is willing to do it."

Jane paused before she nodded. "It can't do any harm to ask," she said. "He is never really off duty; he has too much interest in everything that is going on." She picked up the phone, dialed, and relayed the request to Detective Barker. After a moment she handed the phone to Marge.

"What can I do for you tonight?" he asked.

"Do you know what the status is with Carmella LaCosta? Is she still with the police or, if they let her go, do you know when?"

After a lengthy silence, the detective answered. "I guess it won't do any harm to tell you. The police had nearly finished questioning her in Montesano when I left the station. They said they were bringing her back to Ocean Shores. If they haven't arrived at her hotel yet, they should be there shortly. Dare I ask why?"

"Two things. First, I'd like to get a look at her car, which it turns out is a blue sedan. While I probably won't be able to identify it, I might be able to rule it out. Also, if possible, I'd like to talk with her to fill in a few blanks."

"Looking at the car is a good idea. However, I think you'll remember Miss LaCosta was in police custody at the time someone tried to run you down. Talking to her is something else again. You have no right to interrogate her, but if she is willing to talk with you there is no reason why she can't."

Thanking Jane, they waved goodbye and went to Andrew's car to drive to the Canterbury Inn. "So, it couldn't have been Carmella," Andrew said. "Still, I agree it's better you see the car, especially if it turns out you can eliminate it. Otherwise we'll always be wondering about an accomplice or something."

"True. And I do want to talk with her. All I know about her is what I've heard from all of you."

Carmella's car was still in the lot. Andrew parked beside it. "I'd have stopped for coffee if I'd known we were going to be doing a stakeout," he said.

Marge laughed. "I don't think this would qualify as a stakeout. It should only be a few minutes." She looked over at Carmella's car. "Well, we can't rule out the car on color. It is the right blue. Only Carmella couldn't have been driving it."

She had barely finished speaking when a county police car pulled up behind them. Carmella got out and headed to her car.

"Carmella," Andrew called as he opened his door.

She stopped. "Andrew. What are you doing here?"

"Waiting to talk to you," Andrew said.

"I have nothing to say to you. Don't think that because Craig is dead I want to start up with you again."

"Didn't enter my head," Andrew said. "But, assuming you didn't kill Craig, we'd like to pick your brain to see if you know anything that can help us find out what did happen."

"What's it to you? Or me, for that matter? They've got his wife, don't they?"

"They think they do, but you know Hillary well enough to know she couldn't kill anyone. Marge, here, is trying to clear her of the charges."

Carmella glared at Marge. "I don't suppose you're the one who put the police onto me, are you?"

"Guilty," Marge admitted. "I was worried you would leave before they could find out what you know. And now, since *they* won't tell us anything, we'd like to know also."

"I don't think so," Carmella said. "I've missed a day of work already, and I have nothing to say to you."

"You have to eat," Andrew said. "I'm springing for dinner at Mariah's."

Her face broke into a quizzical smile, followed by a burst of amused laughter. "Outright bribery, huh? Oh, all right, what can it hurt?"

"How did you know Craig would be here this weekend?" Marge asked as soon as they were seated in the restaurant.

"He called me from here. He said he was on vacation at Point Brown this week and under no circumstances should I come. He sounded funny, like he had a cold or something, and I knew he wouldn't care about Hillary knowing if I came. I figured it had to mean he was starting up with another woman and was afraid I'd find out. So much for his promise to divorce Hillary and marry me. I came to see what was going on and to have it out with him."

Andrew was right about one thing, Marge thought. There was no passion in that little speech. If Carmella was telling the truth, she didn't care enough about Craig or about the fact that he was dead to be passionate. What about the lost chance to move into his world?

Carmella had paused for a moment but continued before Marge could think of what to ask her next. "I saw you all at the holiday bazaar. Craig was so angry, I was sure he hadn't been the one who called me. I also knew he would get in contact with me later, to let me know how mad he was."

"What did he do when he left the bazaar, do you know? He never came back inside."

"From where I stood I could see him tear out of the parking lot. There was so much anger in his driving I thought he might have an accident." Her face broke into a wicked grin. "Too bad the murderer wasn't ready to run him off the road. If it looked like an accident no one would have to worry."

"So, he came to your hotel after everyone got home from Aberdeen. That was very late. And he came by the beach? That would make it later yet."

"Yes. He called me on his cell phone when they were in Aberdeen, so I knew he'd be very late. But I had given up and gone to bed before he arrived. When I opened the door to him I was still half asleep. Before I knew it, we ended up in bed together. *Then* he had the gall to tell me that whoever had called me was half right. There was no other woman, but he wouldn't be divorcing his wife to marry me. He said it was my fault we went to bed—I was too tempting all sleepy eyed and tousled. The pig. I'm surprised no one complained to the front desk about the fight that followed his little announcement."

"What time did he get to your place?"

"A little after four o'clock. He said they got home from Aberdeen at three-thirty."

"What time did he leave?"

Carmella frowned. "Must have been between five and five-thirty. I couldn't wait to have him out of there."

"Why didn't you go home that night? Or at least the next morning?"

Carmella's brown eyes were wide when she gazed at Marge. "I have no idea. That would have been the smart thing to do, but I didn't believe Craig and I wanted to know who his new woman was. I suspected he had started up with Anne again, but since they were staying in the same condo I couldn't figure out how I was going to find out for sure. But it would be pretty hard to carry on with someone in the same condo with everyone else—especially since they both had spouses in their bedrooms. I drove down to the resort and hung around for a while, making sure no one saw me.

"I didn't see anything suspicious, and people started coming out to walk the beach, so I went back to the motel. At that point, I was too tired to think of driving back right away, and figured that if I had to pay for another day I might as well use it. Later, when I was eating lunch at the hotel restaurant, I heard about Craig being killed. I couldn't believe it. I was too shocked to think and stayed in my room the rest of the day. Monday morning I decided to snoop around a little and see what I could find out.

"In the end, I decided to stay still another night and leave this morning. Dumb. I should have realized that since you saw me at the bazaar and at the restaurant, sooner or later my name would come up. It was easy for the police to find me. I had checked out and was about to leave this morning when they stopped me. And, that's all I know."

She looked at Andrew. "I hope it was worth the price of the dinner. Now, I want to go home."

"This late?" Marge asked. "The police are finished with you now, so why don't you stay another night and start fresh in the morning?" And why do I care? Marge wondered. Once a mother, always a mother, maybe?

"I want to get out of here, the sooner the better. If I had

done it sooner I wouldn't have had to waste a whole day at the police station. I do have a job. And since I won't be getting married, I'd better make sure I keep it."

Marge couldn't help having a twinge of worry when Carmella drove off, but since the switchbacks through the mountains came in the first half hour of the drive, while she was still fresh, she would probably get home with no problems.

"So, I guess we rule out Carmella?" Andrew asked as they got back into his car for the drive to the resort.

"At least she goes to the end of the line of suspects for now," Marge said. "If she was telling the truth, of course. I wonder why everyone seemed to think she was so hot-blooded? She's as cold as ice."

Andrew laughed. "Like I said, not amorous. Ambitious."

When they returned to Mariner Village, Andrew walked Marge to her door. She turned to him before entering; a strange reluctance to have him leave confused her. "I'd ask you in for a nightcap, but Melissa may be sleeping." Her face warmed. Where had those words come from? Would she have asked if she didn't have an excuse for not following through?

Andrew reached up and tucked a wayward curl behind Marge's ear. His fingers threaded through her hair as he leaned toward her. Marge felt a surge of warmth, a surge of welcome.

The door opened and they jumped apart.

TEN

"PETE PETERSON!" Marge had difficulty keeping her voice steady.

"Marge Christensen," he replied evenly, glaring at Andrew.

"Andrew Barnes," Andrew offered, holding out his hand, apparently oblivious to the currents swirling around them.

Pete hesitated a moment before taking Andrew's hand. When he did, he held onto it in a tight grip a bit longer than necessary for the introduction.

"What are you doing here?" Marge managed.

"I came to see what trouble you were getting into that would make someone try to run you down," Pete answered, his eyes never leaving Andrew's face.

Andrew glanced from one to the other and cleared his throat. Awareness stole over his face. "I guess I should be going." He backed away, turned, and walked rapidly towards the steps.

Pete's steady, deep-gray eyes were unreadable when he turned them to Marge. "Your new admirer?"

"Just an acquaintance." Marge felt her face burn, remembering the sight that had greeted Pete when he opened the door.

Pete shook his head. "I can't leave you alone for a minute," he said. "Remember what happened with your last admirer?"

Before Marge could reply, he swung around and strode after Andrew down the stairs.

Confusion washed over Marge as she stepped into the condo. Melissa sat at the table, toying with a glass of wine, nearly choking in an attempt to keep from laughing. A half finished beer sat on the table across from her.

"You did tell him we were checking on something, didn't you? It wasn't a date," Marge exclaimed.

"Now why would you care if Pete thought it was a date?" Melissa asked. "You are always claiming he is not your detective."

"He isn't my detective. Oh, I don't care. Anyway, what makes him think he needs to check up on me?"

Melissa's face grew serious. "Maybe because he *does* care. About you. I caught a glimpse of you and Andrew in the hall. What was that about?"

Marge flung her arms into the air. "Why do my emotions go haywire with every attractive man I meet?" she wailed.

"Maybe because you're lonely. Maybe because you're too young to deny the possibility of another good relationship."

"Maybe I don't want another good relationship. Not after all the years I neglected my talent for the sake of my family."

"What do you mean, you *neglected* your talent? Weren't you busy raising a family?"

"Yes, I was busy being a wife and a mother. But, I am also

an artist. Why wasn't I developing my talent? How can I be sure I won't neglect it again if I get involved with another man?"

"You weren't developing your talent because you were being the best darn mother you could be. That was what you needed to do then. This is now, a new phase of your life. You can make what you want of it, with or without a man."

Marge sank onto the sofa and sighed. "I don't know. Haven't you ever worried about losing control of your life if you marry David?"

"Frequently," Melissa said, grinning. "Which is why I'm so ready with the answers now." She frowned, as if concentrating on her words. "This is going to sound convoluted, but it is the only conclusion I can reach. I'd never marry a man if I weren't ready to do and be everything he needed. However, I don't know if I could fall in love with a man who wasn't ready to do the same for me." Melissa grinned again. "But, I never had the pleasure of having one man who might have thought we had something started catch me with another man who wanted to start something."

"What would make Pete think we had something started?"

Melissa laughed. "Now, Marge, you can't deny the electricity in the air every time the two of you are together. Why do you think he's been finding reasons to see you even when you aren't involved in one of his investigations?"

"Where is he going now?" Marge wondered aloud, staring at the door. She was surprised by the tears that threatened to spill over at the thought that he might have given up on her; she might never have a chance to explain that she had nothing going on with Andrew.

She didn't, did she?

Why did she have to explain anything to Pete Peterson?

Sleep was hard to come by that night.

For a change, Robert was present when Marge arose on Wednesday morning, but not for long. The police called for him to come in while he and Marge were still savoring their first cups of coffee.

"Robert," Marge ventured before he left, "what can you tell me about your relationship with Hillary? You seem to be spending a lot of time with her, which might make the police look harder at your motives for killing Craig."

"What motives?"

"Oh, I don't know. Your protective instincts, maybe? Getting a vulnerable woman out of an intolerable situation?"

"Really, Mother, you brought me up better than that!"

Marge burst into laughter. Of course she didn't really think Robert could have anything to do with the murder, but if she had any doubts his words might have been enough to dispel it.

"I'm here whether they suspect me or not. Someone has to be here for Hillary."

Marge thought that a lot of people were there for poor little Hillary—all the men, at least. "Tread carefully, Robert. Hillary is in a vulnerable state right now. It would be easy for her to lean on someone else instead of regaining her own strength. It could get complicated, and you could end up involved with her for the wrong reasons."

"I *am* a big boy now, Mother. I can figure these things out for myself."

Oh, sure. That's why he married Caroline.

Shaking her head when Robert was gone, Marge tried to figure out where he really fit in Hillary's life. How and why had they maintained contact over the years? How did it happen that they both came to Ocean Shores at the same time? Why had he felt it was necessary to stay here to be with her? Because she really didn't think the police could have made him stay.

Wandering out to the deck with a second cup of coffee, Marge took a deep breath of the cold salty air and admired the white crests that rose high before crashing down into the surf. Some of the tension seemed to leave her body every time one of the waves came tumbling down.

Her eye caught Hillary and Richard strolling along the beach. Their heads were down as if deep in thought and their shoulders almost touched. Marge grinned. Perhaps, given time, her worries about Kate and Robert's involvement with the Point Brown contingent would disappear on their own. Maybe her involvement would disappear, too.

From the right she caught sight of Anne in a green sweat suit jogging through the sand, arms pumping at her sides.

Rushing back into the condo, Marge grabbed her sketchpad and pencil. When she returned to the deck Anne was nearly out of sight. No problem. Marge sat down and drew what she had seen. She knew her fingers wouldn't forget. She again drew the woman she had seen jogging when she was walking back from the jetty. She frowned. Were they the same? They were certainly similar, but Marge wasn't sure, and normally she would be. Was she losing her touch?

"Melissa, what do you think of these two figures?" Marge asked, being careful not to hint what she thought Melissa would see.

"Looks like the same person wearing different outfits," Melissa said, peering over Marge's shoulder. She cocked her head. "Is this Anne? She must also have a pink sweat suit."

Marge nodded. "If you're right, that means it was probably Anne I saw the afternoon I was drawing at the jetty, not Hillary. I'm not sure though."

"Well, even if you were sure, I don't think the police would take your drawings as any kind of proof."

"No, but it backs up that we can't identify Hillary from the drawings. It could as easily have been Anne."

The police still had her sketches of the woman she had seen push Craig and speed-walk away from him. From what she could remember, that was the same person she had seen jogging. So it could have been Anne both times.

"Oh, no," Marge said. "I forgot to ask Carmella if she owned a pink sweat suit. Or if she saw Craig on the beach before they ran into each other at the bazaar." She frowned. "From Craig's reaction, it seemed like the first time he saw Carmella was at the bazaar. But he could have ordered her to leave Ocean Shores and his reaction was anger at seeing her hanging around."

Marge picked up the phone and dropped it. Did she want to continue working with Andrew on this? She paced the room. What if Pete found them together again? She shook her head. Despite what Melissa said, Pete had never indicated he was interested in her in a personal way. Besides, to get the answers she needed, she had no choice. She picked up the phone again and punched in the number before she could change her mind.

"Good morning."

"Andrew. Good morning to you, too. I'm glad you're not out on the beach with everyone else. I have a question."

"I hope I have an answer." His voice was guarded.

"Do you have a number where I can get in touch with Carmella? I forgot to ask her one important question last night."

"I have a number. I'm not sure she would appreciate my giving it out without her permission. Can I ask her the question?"

Marge hesitated. Hearing Carmella's tone of voice might mean as much as her answer, but Marge couldn't fault Andrew for guarding private information. If she had Andrew ask Carmella to call her back, would Carmella do it? It wasn't worth the risk. "All I want to know is if she has a pink sweat suit and, if she does, did she see Craig on the beach while wearing it."

"I don't think she said she saw Craig on the beach."

"No, but people don't always tell you things if you don't think to ask." Or if they think it might not be the wisest thing to do, she thought. "She may have forgotten to mention it, as zeroed in as she was on their big fight at the motel."

"It won't hurt to ask her. I'll call right now in case she slept in, but I may not be able to reach her until this evening if she went to work already."

"You can't call her at work?"

"No. Carmella was very protective of that part of her life. I guess she knew she upset a lot of people and she didn't want them intruding on her workplace. She leaves her cell phone in the car when she is at work."

"Okay, thanks. Let me know if you find out anything," Marge said, and hung up. What now? She had no idea how to continue this investigation—and time was getting short.

Frowning, she chewed on her lower lip. She shouldn't concentrate too much on the sweat suits. Even if all three women owned pink sweat suits and wore them this weekend, which would be a strange coincidence, that didn't mean one of them killed Craig. And it was cold enough to wear a hat on the beach; there was no reason to think doing so was an attempt to conceal one's identity.

"Well, I'm at my wits end with this thing. What would you like to do today?" Marge asked Melissa when she finally emerged from her bedroom.

"Let's take a walk on the beach before breakfast. Never can tell who might show up there." The look of innocence on Melissa's face didn't fool Marge at all.

"Sounds good," she said. Melissa was headed for disappointment if she thought they would run into Pete Peterson. He was undoubtedly back at his desk in Bellevue by now.

They both pulled on sweatshirts and ear warmers to combat the wind, which seemed to blow harder and colder today. Clambering down the loose embankment, they trudged through soft sand to reach the firm damp sand near the surf, but far enough back to avoid the water that surged beneath the waves, pushing farther and farther up the beach with each encroachment before suddenly dropping back. They hadn't gone far before they ran into Anne, jogging towards Point Brown.

"You sure own a lot of different colored sweat suits," Marge said. "Blue and pink and green. And you brought them all for one week at the beach."

Anne grinned. "I am a bit of a clothes horse, aren't I? But I don't own a pink sweat suit. It doesn't suit my coloring. Pink is better on Hillary."

Marge frowned. Was Anne lying? Well, she would, wouldn't she, if she were guilty? She would have worn the pink sweat suit in order to make anyone watching think it was Hillary, because she was right about pink not suiting her carroty red hair. The mistake she made, if it was her, was jogging and speed walking instead of copying Hillary's defeatist gait. And, she would have had to make her plan before coming to Ocean Shores and bought a pink sweat suit in order to look like Hillary. How would Anne have known Hillary would come with a pink sweat suit? Did they talk beforehand? Not likely, but she could ask Hillary.

Marge sighed. What difference did it make if Anne had a pink sweat suit and lied about it? She had an alibi. She was with Kate all night the night Craig was killed. So, did Carmella jog and speed walk also? Another question for Andrew to ask her. And if she did, would she look like Hillary? Carmella was tall and willowy, too, so she could probably pass for Hillary at a distance, if you couldn't see the skin coloring.

Anne took off to continue her jog while Marge and Melissa trudged into the wind for another ten minutes.

"I need a break from this," Melissa said. "My nose is getting numb and my cheeks will be frostbitten before long. Let's walk twenty minutes the other way, with the wind to our backs. That way it will only be another ten into the wind to return to the condo."

Twenty minutes later they stopped and looked at each other. "I guess we have no choice but to brave the wind if we want to get back to the condo, so let's go for it," Marge said. "Could you hold the fort at the condo for a while? I need to go speak with Hillary about something, and the police might finish with Robert before I get back. I don't want him to leave the condo until I can talk to him."

Melissa grinned. "Nothing like a good walk to get the juices flowing again. Sure, take your time."

When they reached the condo, Marge grabbed her car keys and drove over to the Point Brown Resort, unwilling to spend any more time out in the weather. As usual, Andrew answered the door.

"Is Hillary here?" Marge asked.

"Yes," Hillary's voice came from the background. "Is Robert with you?"

"No, he's with the police," Marge said, trying to hide the worry in her voice. "Are both Anne and John still out?"

"Yes, again," Andrew answered. "Now you have me curious. We're having a cup of coffee. Come on in and join us. Do you mind if I sit in?"

"Not at all," Marge said as she sat at the table and accepted a steaming cup. "Hillary, did you discuss wardrobe with Anne at all before coming here?"

"No," Hillary said, her face reflecting puzzlement.

"So she would have no way of knowing you were bringing a pink sweat suit. Did you ever see her in a pink sweat suit?"

Hillary shook her head. "Blue and green. That's all I've seen her wear. The green looks best on her."

Marge bit at her lower lip. "Do you lock your bedroom doors when you are not in the rooms?"

"No again. Where is this going, Marge?" Andrew asked.

Marge chewed a moment longer. "What did you usually do when Craig went out by himself?" she asked Hillary.

"Read in the living room or, if it was warm enough, out on the deck. Sometimes I would go sit in the hot tub for a while."

"So, it would be easy enough for someone to go into your room, take your pink sweat suit, and wear it, then come back and return it without your knowing."

"Why would someone do that?" she asked. "Oh, you mean the two times you thought you saw me on the beach but it wasn't me. You think it was Anne?"

"Maybe. But I can't figure out why. She has an alibi for when Craig was killed, so she wouldn't need to throw suspicion on you. Anyway, if that were what she was doing, why would she portray you more physically fit than you are?"

Hillary stared out the window. "I do remember coming in one time and thinking my sweat suit wasn't put away very neatly. I am usually fastidious about how I treat my clothes, so I notice things like that. I thought I must have been upset and careless."

"If Anne borrowed Hillary's sweat suit," Andrew said, "there might be some of her red hair or other evidence on it. Should we look at it?"

Marge shook her head. "The less we handle it the better. I don't think the county police will look at it either, but I'll call Detective Barker and see if I can talk him into it."

"Here," Andrew said, handing her a phone. "Do it now."

"Well, I'm curious," Detective Barker said when she reached him. "I agree the woman in your sketches didn't have Mrs. Carlson's bearing. You don't have much to go on, though. Let me call the county guys and see what they think. I'll call you right back."

Marge gave him the number and hung up. True to his word, the detective called back in fifteen minutes.

"The county guys think it's a waste of time and money, so they won't go for it. However, they have no objection to me taking a look, and I might as well bag whatever I find in case something changes later."

"Great," Marge said. "Thank you."

She called Melissa to fill her in and discovered Robert had arrived and was anxious to check up on Hillary. "We'll drive over to Point Brown in Robert's car," Melissa said. They arrived a few minutes later.

"Have you made any headway on finding the car that tried to run you down?" Andrew asked.

"I've had a thought about that car," Melissa said.

All eyes turned to her.

"This is wild, but we couldn't figure out why the killer would try to run down Marge when that would only draw attention away from Hillary. What if it wasn't the killer? What if someone else wanted to create a distraction that would draw attention away from Hillary, without getting involved and maybe throwing suspicion on him or herself?"

"Or," Marge said, picking up the thought, "what if it was the killer but he or she didn't want Hillary to take the blame? Maybe he or she was trying to create a smokescreen, drawing attention away from Hillary.

"Wow," Andrew said. "So this is how it works. In one minute you've been able to come up with two plausible reasons why that person tried to run you down. Or at least, seemed to."

"Right," Marge said. "There is no reason to think the driver wanted to kill me. I assumed he or she wanted to scare me off, but I don't know enough for that to make any sense. It could have been simply to draw suspicion away from Hillary."

"In which case, I could have done it myself," Hillary said. "Except, I didn't. And I don't have a blue car."

Detective Barker arrived. They all watched as he pulled on a pair of surgical type gloves and followed Hillary into her room. He came back with a plastic bag and brought it over to show Marge.

"That blonde hair is probably mine," Hillary said. "Those two others look like Anne's."

"My what?" Anne's voice demanded as she charged through the door and pushed Robert aside to see what they were talking about. John entered behind her and disappeared into their bedroom. "What are all of you doing here? I hope you aren't going through my things or you'll have a lot of trouble on your hands."

"Not your things. Hillary's. Her pink sweat suit, to be precise. Which for some reason has a few strands of hair around the collar that look a lot like yours," Detective Barker said.

"So what? We're living in the same condo. That could have come from anywhere. Besides, even if I had borrowed her sweat suit, which I didn't, what would it prove? I was with Kate when Craig was killed, so I couldn't have killed him. End of story."

Detective Barker cocked his head at Marge. She was afraid that meant Anne had a point about the hairs coming from anywhere, as well as her unbreakable alibi.

"Thank you for coming over yesterday, Robert," Hillary said, breaking the silence. "I needed someone to help keep my mind off all of this." Marge felt a prickle at the back of her neck. Why did Hillary have to wait until this exact moment to note Robert's presence and his attention to her?

Detective Barker looked at Robert with narrowed eyes, and then glanced around the room. "And how did *you* become that person?" he asked. "It seems to me there are several people here able to fill the bill."

ELEVEN

RICHARD EMERGED from a bedroom, startling Marge. She hadn't realized he had also returned to the condo.

"I just got off the phone with the office," Richard said. "They decided to get an attorney for Hillary; he is going to Montesano to talk to the county police. After that he'll come and talk to us. I expect that will be late this afternoon, since he hasn't left Seattle yet. Marge, since you've been looking into all of this, it might be good if you were around to fill him in on anything that might help clear Hillary."

"I'll be glad to, though I have more questions than answers. In fact, the questions keep proliferating and the answers I come up with don't fit any of them."

Detective Barker laughed. "Welcome to the world of investigation. I think I'll take my little baggie and go back to the office."

Anne's blue eyes shot icicles at his back. When the door

closed behind him, she sliced them toward Marge. "If you have any more questions about pink sweat suits, you better talk to Carmella. I'm sure I saw her out on the beach in one, because it surprised me. She doesn't usually wear pastel colors. From now on I'll thank you to leave me out of your amateur sleuthing." She went into her room and slammed the door.

Richard took Hillary's arm. "Hillary needs a break from all this," he said. "I'm taking her up the coast for lunch at a nice little restaurant. After that we might take a drive, but we'll be back in time to meet with the attorney."

Robert looked stunned as he watched them leave; hurt and confusion washed across his face. Swallowing hard, Marge bit back a reminder that she had warned him.

"Hillary will always have people to look after her," Andrew said, his voice gentle. "I'm sorry if you felt you had to stay here to do that." Marge shot him a grateful smile.

Robert blinked. It seemed to take an effort to pull himself together enough to answer. "No, of course not," he said, his voice gruff. "I thought . . . well, I did think she needed me, actually."

Robert had never been good at hiding his feelings, and it was obvious to Marge that there was more to them than he said, even though she didn't want to admit it. She had a few questions for him the next time they were alone. But she had to tuck that into a back corner of her mind right now in order to stay on track. "What color car does Richard drive?" she asked.

"He drives a yellow Volvo," Andrew said. "Not the car you're looking for. Good thinking, though. He could fit your idea of someone trying to protect Hillary by drawing attention away from her." He glanced at Robert quickly—but not so fast that Marge missed the implication.

"And, John and Anne have a white car, if I remember

correctly. You have a light-blue car," Marge added, looking at Andrew. She glanced at Robert. What time had he arrived in Ocean Shores? What time did he spend with Hillary? But, Robert? Running his mother down to muddy the waters? Impossible. If only she could be sure the police would see it that way. She certainly wasn't going to be the one to draw attention to the color of Robert's car.

"So, no one has a dark-blue car like the one that ran us down except Carmella, and she was with the police when it happened. Nothing is adding up." She sighed. "Well, we might as well go home and figure out what we're going to do with the rest of our day. We're not making any headway here."

"We all need a break," Andrew declared. "Why don't we take a page from Richard's book and have a change of scenery? We could drive to Lake Quinault. It's about an hour and a half away, but the Lodge and a late lunch in the Roosevelt Dining Room are worth the drive. We can choose from several walking trails through the rainforest depending on how long we want to stay, and still be back in time to meet the attorney."

Marge hesitated. If Hillary had acquired a new protector, Robert might not be as concerned about helping her, so maybe Marge could relax and enjoy the rest of the week. But, no, she couldn't relax; not as long as there was a chance something could come back to bite Robert.

"You three go ahead," Robert said. "I think I'll go back to the condo and crash."

Marge almost smiled. The opportunity to talk with Robert had dropped in her lap. "No. If you don't go, I don't go. Being alone isn't what you need right now, and I'd rather spend my time with you."

Robert attempted a smile, but it fell short. "Thanks,

Mom, but I haven't slept well the last couple of days so I wouldn't be very good company. If I go back to the condo, I'll probably be dead to the world before long."

"Okay," Marge said. "You take a nap and when you wake up we'll have some time together."

Robert gave her a crooked grin. "There's no arguing with her when she's in Mom mode," he commented to the room at large. "I don't want to rob you of a chance to have a little vacation, and there is nothing you can do here with everyone gone, so let's go to Lake Quinault. I can sleep on the way."

"Poor kid," Melissa whispered when Robert preceded them out the door. "For such a nice, good-looking guy he has the worst luck with women."

"He may not have good instincts about them, but he got one benefit out of this episode," Andrew said.

"What's that?" Marge asked.

"He got rid of that simpering gold digger he brought with him."

"Really, Andrew!" Marge protested. "I admit I wasn't sorry to see that relationship didn't come to anything, but how can you categorize Ruthie that way when you hardly knew her?"

"The way she came on to Craig, while she supposedly was crazy about Robert. She was looking for the main chance, the same way Carmella was. She wasn't as direct or skilled at it, that's all."

Marge was tempted to agree with Andrew's assessment, given the different person Ruthie had become after giving up on Robert. But she didn't live in Ruthie's skin and couldn't know what made Ruthie act as she did. Besides, she had come to the reluctant conclusion that Robert had used Ruthie for window dressing. He had never shown any real interest in her, only Hillary. Marge wondered again if he had known Hillary would be here before he arranged for the condo. She needed to have that talk with him. First, though, she had to figure out how to get him to open up.

Overcast skies and incessant drizzle accompanied their drive to Lake Quinault but the change of scenery did lighten their spirits. By the time they settled in the historic Roosevelt Dining Room at the Lodge, they were more than ready for the warmth of the rich and filling clam chowder served for lunch.

The dining room was named for the president who in 1938 signed a bill creating the Olympic National Forest. A wall of windows provided a wide view of the lake and the mountain looming close to the water on the other side. After admiring the huge fireplace and "men's club" ambience of the lobby area, they stopped by the Ranger station to get some information about the rainforest and the trails.

They had a choice of several, ranging in length from a quarter of a mile to twenty miles and labeled with four degrees of difficulty. After looking over the material, they decided to start with a quarter mile hike to see the world's largest Sitka Spruce, a type of tree that only grew in the Northwest. Next, they would drive over to the nearby Gatton Creek loop, which was about a mile and a half of relatively easy terrain. That was probably all they could manage and still return to Ocean Shores before Hillary's attorney arrived.

"When Robert and Kate were small, my husband and I took them through the Hoh rainforest further north on the Olympic Peninsula. It always amazes me to have rainforest in this temperate zone. I think of it as a tropical phenomenon."

"Caused by mild temperatures, lots of rain, and summer fog," Andrew read from a brochure. "This is one of the last temperate zone rain forests in existence," he added.

"Lots of rain is right," Melissa said, laughing, as the wind picked up and blew moisture off the trees onto them. She looked up and gasped. "Can you believe the height of some of these trees? They shoot straight up into the heavens."

Looking ahead as they came to the end of the short trail, they all stood in wonder. "Fifty-eight feet eleven inches in girth and one hundred ninety-one feet tall," Andrew read. After admiring the mammoth Sitka Spruce and snapping pictures from every direction, they drove to the trailhead for the Gatton Creek loop. After a few minutes on the trail, Marge dropped back to walk with Robert, who had started lagging behind.

"I told you I wouldn't be good company," he said.

Marge checked to be sure the others were well ahead of them before speaking in a low voice. "Okay, Robert, I want some answers now."

His head jerked up, his brown eyes startled. "Answers? About what?"

"Lots of things," Marge said, scuffling the damp leaves that blanketed the path. "Like, how did you happen to get the same week as Hillary to come to the shore? And why? And how closely did you stay in contact with her after your divorce?"

Only birdsong and a whisper of wind disturbed the quiet of the forest. Waiting Robert out, Marge admired the juxtaposition of evergreen and bare trees. She had to hide a grin. Mom mode for sure.

Marge thought it was the peace and quiet that finally freed Robert to talk. "You're right," he said. "When I heard Hillary and the gang were coming here this week I paid a friend to use his timeshare credits to come at the same time. There was no award from work.

"Hillary called me a couple of months ago, asking to

meet for coffee. I agreed. When I saw her, I couldn't believe the difference. She was so thin, so listless, compared to what she had been before." He stopped for a moment, a faraway look in his eyes that told Marge he had been attracted to Hillary's former self.

"She told me about her marriage. She said she'd always liked and trusted me; she said she thought Caroline was crazy to let me go. When she asked for my advice, I didn't know what to say. She told me they were coming to Ocean Shores and that one of Craig's women intended to get him to marry her. Because he had no intention to divorce Hillary, she was afraid the woman might try to get rid of her. That sounded pretty farfetched to me, but there was no question she was desperate. In the end, I told Hillary I would see what I could do and started looking for a way to join her here. I didn't have a week of vacation, and I did have those meetings, but I figured if I brought you here you would keep an eye on her."

"It sounds like you were attracted to her."

Robert squeezed his eyes shut for a moment. "Yeah, I guess I was. Am. And I was flattered that she turned to me. Only now it looks like I'm totally unneeded."

Marge reached out and touched his arm. "Maybe she felt more secure with you than with any of Craig's coworkers. But Richard is a sympathetic guy, and he seems willing to provide a shoulder for her to lean on. As I told you before, she is in a vulnerable state, and you can't read too much into her need for support. The problem is your feelings for Hillary do give you a motive for killing Craig."

Robert stopped short. "Mom, you can't believe that. You can't think I had anything to do with Craig's death."

"No, of course I don't. But I know you; I know how easy it is to provoke your protective instinct. The police don't. That is why I think it's a bad idea that you stayed, as it only emphasizes that you care for Hillary. You need to be careful about how much time you spend with her."

"I still want to help her," Robert said, his chin getting the stubborn look Marge knew so well. "I can't let her be accused of murder when she couldn't have done it."

Wet splashes on her face made Marge look up. Melissa turned and beckoned for them to hurry and catch up. Fortunately, it was only a light mist so they all managed a mad dash that completed the loop back to the car without getting completely soaked. They welcomed the warm atmosphere of Lake Quinault Lodge while they dried off and drank coffee around the fireplac.

"I'm glad we managed to put a little more vacation into your week, Melissa," Marge said. "But now we need to get back to Ocean Shores to see the attorney, and so Andrew can call Carmella. We still have a few questions to clear up."

The drive back was quiet as they were all lost in their own thoughts.

So, Hillary said she felt threatened by a woman who wanted Craig. Marge frowned. Would that have been Carmella? Marge could believe Carmella might kill Craig in a fit of jealousy or rage, but would she kill him in cold blood? And why had Hillary chosen Robert to be her protector rather than one of the men who were in the condo with her? When Marge looked at Robert out of the corner of her eye, she suspected that she knew why. Tall and strong, and with soft, brown eyes full of care and concern, he appeared to be the answer for any damsel in distress.

When the four of them arrived at Ocean shores, Richard and Hillary had not yet returned from their trip.

"I didn't think to ask you, do you know if Carmella jogs or speed walks?" Marge asked Andrew as he poured wine for her and Melissa.

"I don't know," he said, taking a can of beer for himself

and offering one to Robert. "She works out at the gym, and there's no reason why she couldn't, but I've never seen her doing it."

"Well, if she's athletic she probably knows the moves of a jogger. It would be good to know if she brought a pink sweat suit with her, though how we'd find out if she doesn't tell us is beyond me. Also—although this is a bit of a stretch—it would help to know if anyone else has keys to her car." She shook her head. "We are missing something or some connection, because otherwise this whole thing makes no sense at all."

As soon as it was late enough for Carmella to be out of work, Andrew phoned her. Carmella agreed to talk with Marge one last time.

"Did you bring a pink sweat suit with you to Ocean Shores?" Marge asked.

"No, I don't own a pink sweat suit," Carmella said. "I don't like pastel colors."

"Did you spend any time walking or running on the beach?"

"Not really. I used the workout room and walked for a bit on the beach, but I stayed pretty close to the Canterbury Inn."

"Does anyone else have access to your car keys?"

"No. I'm very careful about that. I had a car totaled once by a so-called friend who had borrowed it without my permission; I've kept my keys secure ever since."

Marge was shaking her head when she hung up the phone. "Carmella might not be telling the truth, and she is the only one with no alibi for the time Craig was killed. While her motive is weak, it's about as good as anyone else's. She has a temper and she is the only one with a dark-blue car. But we have nothing to really tie her to the murder and she has a rock solid alibi for when the car nearly ran us down. I hardly know where to go from here."

"You're not giving up, are you, Mom?" Robert asked, anxiety in his voice.

"No, of course not," she answered. "After all this time we haven't eliminated anybody. We're still left with Anne, John, Richard, Carmella, and you, Andrew. Of you four, Anne appears to be the best suspect. She may have 'borrowed' Hillary's pink sweat suit and had an altercation with Craig while she was wearing it.

"But she was with Kate during the whole period when Craig was killed."

"Leaving Richard, John, Carmella, and me?" Andrew asked. "I don't think Richard was worried enough about his job to murder for it, but he might be someone who would create the distraction of running you down in order to make everyone think the killer was still out there while Carmella was with the police. Of course, he'd have to get a dark-blue car from somewhere. He could have rented one, I suppose, as any one of us could have, but that would be easy enough for the police to trace."

Marge jumped up and grabbed the phone, dialing the number for the Ocean Shores Police Department. "That car running us down was in your jurisdiction, wasn't it?" she asked, relieved that Detective Barker was still at the station.

"Yes, it was."

"Would you consider checking the car rental places in the area? I think it should include the local airport, Aberdeen, Hoquiam, Montesano, and probably even Westport—to see if anyone rented a dark-blue car?"

"Whoa, any number of people could have done that," said Detective Barker.

"But we're only interested in whether someone in our

group of suspects did. If not, we can eliminate more people from driving the car."

"I think it's worth a shot. I'll get someone on it right now. The better I get to know you, Mrs. Christensen, the more I understand Pete Peterson's respect for you."

Marge felt a warm glow at the secondhand praise from Pete, before she remembered he had walked out in a way that made her fear he had no more interest in her. She sat back down and gazed at Andrew.

"Hey," he said. "You're not rehashing all the reasons I might have done it, are you?"

"No," she said, her voice thoughtful. "I'm thinking about Carmella. She says a man called her claiming to be Craig. That's why she was here, but Craig said he didn't call." Marge gazed at Robert. Would the police suspect that *he* was the one who called Carmella? Why would he, or anyone, do that? Carmella had a dark-blue car, which the caller must have known and might have been able to get into. Maybe Carmella was the one being framed for the murder and the ax fell on Hillary, instead. "But why was the gun in Hillary's room?" Marge was startled to realize she had spoken the last sentence aloud.

"It was Craig's gun, remember?" Andrew said. "The killer may not have realized their room would be searched, though why they wouldn't have realized Hillary would be the prime suspect, I don't know. And, not being a professional, the killer probably didn't know how to get into Carmella's motel room to plant the gun there."

"Or," Robert said, "the killer could have figured if getting Carmella to Ocean Shores didn't work out, then making Hillary the prime suspect was a fallback."

"But, why would the killer try to take attention away from Hillary by running us down in what looked like Carmella's car?" Marge rubbed her forehead, which was beginning to ache. "We're going in circles. The only other thing I can think of is that whoever tried to run us down did not know Carmella was being interrogated by the police at that time. They might have been making a last-ditch effort to throw suspicion on her."

"That makes sense," Andrew said.

"So, we think Carmella could have been set up by who-ever killed Craig, and that person doesn't want Hillary to take the blame," Robert said. "Now, what do we do about it?"

Good question, Marge thought as they all stared at her son. Who wouldn't want Hillary to take the blame—other than Robert? Her eyes slid over to Andrew. At this point only Richard and Andrew seemed to be viable suspects. She didn't want to believe it was Andrew, and if she didn't, that left Richard.

"Okay," Marge said. "Let's consider Richard. Who can account for his movements from the time you got back from Aberdeen until after Craig was killed? And, for the time the car ran us down?"

"I only know he did come back to the condo Saturday night," Andrew said. "I heard him saying goodnight and coming into our room. But I slept soundly most of the night, so I don't know if he stayed until morning. I didn't hear Craig go back out, either."

Marge pressed her fingers against the sides of her fore-head. "That has been bothering me. Why did Anne get Kate to watch the sunrise with her? Wouldn't you think she would have done that with her husband?"

"Anne and John were squabbling all evening and he said he'd rather go to bed than watch the sunrise," Robert said. "He looked beat, and we were all tired, but he could have simply been too angry to want to go with her."

Marge started to ask about the bickering, but decided

they needed to get back to Richard. "At what time Sunday morning did anyone see Richard?"

"I saw him at eight," Andrew said. "Hillary and Carmella both say Craig went to see Carmella and left there in the early morning hours. He must have been killed on his way back to the condo, before daylight; otherwise the killer risked being seen since a lot of people take early morning walks on the beach. Sunrise is around seven these days. Richard would have had time to do it, get back to the condo, and be in bed when I got up at eight." He shook his head. "But I would swear he was sound asleep, and it looked like he had been that way for some time. Besides, I don't sleep that soundly early in the morning and I would think I would have awakened if Richard came into the room anytime after six."

"The killer probably had no way of knowing when Craig would return from Carmella's motel," Marge said. "But, if he knew when Craig left the condo, he would know he had at least an hour or two, so he could wait for Craig on the beach—or in the dune grass above the beach," she added, remembering the flattened grass she had noticed while painting the scene.

"Did we ever find out what time Craig left Carmella's motel?" Melissa asked.

"Carmella said it was between five and five-thirty," Marge answered. "I wonder if the police checked at the motel to see if anyone could verify that."

"Five to five-thirty," Andrew said. "So, if that's right, we know Craig was killed sometime after that, probably closer to six to allow him time to walk to where he was found, and probably before seven o'clock."

"Any idea what the tide level was Sunday morning?" Melissa asked.

"Another good question," Marge said. "I'll ask Jane." When she hung up the phone a few minutes later she announced, "Low tide was at about five-thirty in the morning, and the next high tide wasn't until around noon, so that doesn't change our time frame." She took a deep breath. "Okay, let's start at the beginning again. You all returned from Aberdeen at about three-thirty. Robert and Ruthie came directly to Mariner Village. I know because Robert's cell phone rang after they got in. Kate and Anne made coffee and went back out to talk for a few hours and watch the sunrise. They both returned to the condos at about seven-thirty."

Marge paused for a moment, trying to make sure all those people were eliminated. "That was an awfully long conversation between Kate and Anne, but I guess the alcohol loosened their tongues. I hope you all agree Kate has nothing to do with this and that she can vouch for Anne?"

Seeing nods all around, Marge looked at Robert. "And, we can assume Ruthie went straight to bed," she added, looking at Robert.

"She did," he answered; the others nodded in agreement.

"So, who called you at three-thirty in the morning?" Marge asked.

Robert stepped back as if to avoid the question. With everyone waiting, expectant, he finally answered. "Hillary called to tell me Craig had gone out. She said she was nervous and asked if I could come over. I was half asleep already, so I told her I thought she could trust Andrew and Richard to watch out for her."

Marge frowned. That didn't even make as much sense as Hillary asking Robert to stay at Ocean Shores. She'd have to ask Hillary what she was thinking. A slight chill went up her back when she realized she had gone to sleep right after the call. No one could prove Robert hadn't gone out, after all.

"Richard and Hillary both arrived at Point Brown with

Craig, and about the same time as John, so I assume they can all vouch for each other," Marge continued. "Andrew was already asleep; Richard can vouch for that.

"So, everyone got home. But maybe everyone didn't stay. I know Robert and Ruthie were both asleep at six o'clock when I got up. We don't know if everyone was in your condo until you got up at eight, right Andrew? At that time, you know Richard was in the condo, but you have no way to verify if anyone was in the other bedrooms. Did you see Anne come in?"

"No. But I heard someone come in before I got up. I assume it was Anne since that was about the same time Kate got home."

Marge shook her head. "If we rule out Hillary, we're back to Richard and you, Andrew."

"And John," Melissa said.

Marge looked at her.

"You keep leaving out John. You haven't thought much about whether he might have found out about Craig and Anne, and how it would have affected him, have you?" Melissa asked.

Marge shook her head. "Anne warned me off the one time I mentioned any chance John might be involved, and I really never thought about him again. How could I have let it go at that?" She turned to Andrew. "How well do you know John?"

"Not well at all. I only saw him at office functions that included spouses, and he never talked or mingled, mainly stayed back in a corner nursing a beer."

"Did anyone else get to know him? Like Richard?"

"Not that I could see."

"If Andrew was awake enough to hear Anne come in at seven-thirty or so, is it likely he would have heard anyone come in after six?" Melissa asked.

They all looked at Andrew, who was frowning in thought. "I think so. I begin waking up early and doze lightly for an hour or two before actually getting out of bed. I think I would have heard anyone after five or six."

"What if . . ." Marge paused to clear her thoughts.

"Yes?" the others chorused.

"What if Anne and John were in it together? Anne established an alibi by watching the sunrise with Kate. She met up with John after he killed Craig. They returned to the condo together, making as little noise as possible, and if anyone heard something they would think it was only Anne coming in because the time was right for her to be getting home after dropping off Kate at Mariner Village."

"There she goes again," Melissa said, a wide grin on her face.

"If we think that's what happened," said Marge, "we have to figure out how they got Craig's gun and why Anne faked impersonating Hillary on the beach, because that certainly wasn't a real effort to make anyone think it was Hillary. And we need to find out if and how they obtained a blue car to run us down. And, if we manage all that, of course, we still have to figure out how to prove it."

TWELVE

M ARGE BEGAN TO pace the room, feeling excitement bubbling inside her. "Let's take a closer look at those two. In addition to being sexually abused, Anne's business life and personal life were threatened by Craig. John has a stake in both. John could have called Carmella, impersonating Craig, to get Carmella to the beach so they could put the blame on her. Anne could have impersonated Carmella impersonating Hillary."

"Why would she do that?" Melissa asked.

"They wanted to make it look like Carmella had more contact with Craig than she admitted when questioned; thus Anne impersonated Hillary on the beach. And, if that didn't work, they could catch Hillary in what looked like a lie, the way I assumed at first, which would tend to make Hillary look guilty.

"Anyway, John has been slinking around distracted, like

someone with something on his mind. These are not sea-soned criminals, after all. He would probably have a strong reaction to having killed someone."

"They could have manufactured their quarreling in order to throw people off track," Melissa added.

"I wonder if Detective Barker has found out about the rental yet," Robert said. "If it turns out Anne or John rented a dark-blue car, we would have our answer."

As if on cue, the phone rang. "No luck on the rental," Detective Barker said. "No rentals by anyone in your group, and no rentals at all of a dark-blue sedan."

"Well, there goes the easy answer," Marge said when she hung up. "Where are Anne and John right now?"

"Not in their room," Andrew said after knocking on their door and peeking in.

"We still haven't found the hat worn by the woman who impersonated Hillary on the beach," Marge said.

"We can't look in their room!" Andrew exclaimed. All of them looked at Marge expectantly.

She shrugged, pretending a nonchalance she didn't feel. "I can look without taking anything. Someone needs to keep an eye out for their return."

"That'll be me," Melissa said, slipping down to the lower level.

Marge took a long-handled spoon and a sheet of paper towel from the kitchen and went to the door of the bed-room. She could have cried with dismay. There were so many places where the hat could be out of sight and she didn't want to disturb anything to the point Anne would know she had been in the room.

Entering quietly, as if Anne might hear her, she opened the closet door using the paper towel to prevent leaving fin-gerprints. When she realized what she was doing, she had

155

to stifle a laugh. Too many detective stories, for sure. Why would anyone be checking for fingerprints in Anne's room?

There was nothing on the floor or the overhead rack. She used the spoon to move clothes back and forth. Nothing. The suitcase on the floor was closed. That would need to be opened if her search of the easier places came up empty. After kneeling to peer under the bed, she used the spoon to lift each pillow high enough to see under it. No hat appeared there or in the drawers of the bedside tables. She started at the top drawer of the dresser and used the spoon to gently search among the items in each drawer. In the bottom drawer, she hit pay dirt.

"It's there," she said after leaving the room and closing the door. "Not even very well hidden. That could explain why Anne was so upset when we found her hair on the suit and she thought we had gone into their room. I wonder why she didn't destroy it. Or take it with her when she left?"

"She probably didn't think she would ever come under suspicion," Andrew said. "And even if she did, how would the police get enough corroboration to get a search warrant?"

Melissa came back into the condo. "Anne and John are coming. They drove up in two cars."

Marge frowned. "One of them isn't dark blue, is it?"

Melissa laughed. "It could never be that easy. It looks like they rented a white Toyota. Why would they need two cars though?"

Anne looked around with suspicion when she and John entered the condo. They both went into their room without saying a word.

Hillary and Richard appeared at the open door, followed by a balding, somewhat rotund man Marge decided must be Hillary's attorney.

"Frank Wiens," he said. "I will be representing Hillary

Carlson if she is arrested for her husband's murder. I would like to talk with each one of you, if I may."

The condo suddenly felt crowded. Richard, Hillary, and Andrew went to their rooms so the attorney could talk with Robert and Marge. They had barely sat down in the living area and begun the interview when Anne burst out of her bedroom, holding the pink knit hat up high.

"Who put this in my room?" she demanded. "It does not belong to me." Turning an accusing eye on Marge while the other bedroom doors opened, she said, "I told you, I don't wear pink. Someone is trying to make me look guilty—first those hairs on Hillary's sweat suit and now this."

What a great act, Marge thought. And where was John? Hiding in the bedroom?

Anne threw the hat across the room, turned, and stomped back into the bedroom, slamming the door behind her.

"We think those two are the guilty ones," Marge said, and outlined how they had come to that conclusion.

"Very good reasoning," said the attorney. "Remember, we don't have to prove they did it. We only have to prove they could have done it as easily and had as much motive as Hillary. Any other suspects we can throw into the mix?"

The others, lured by Anne's outburst, had joined them. "Well, there's Craig's mistress Carmella LaCosta," said Andrew. "She's been around this weekend, too, and word is Craig was throwing her over after promising to marry her."

"Excellent," said the attorney. "I don't think we'll have a thing to worry about." Nevertheless, he continued his questioning of all of them, before knocking on the Jacobs' door.

"We don't have anything to say to you," Anne said. "I'm sure that busybody Marge Christensen has filled you in on all the gory details and made me out to be the killer. Did she neglect to tell you I was with her daughter at the time of the murder?"

"I may have to get a subpoena for a deposition," the attorney warned.

"You do that," Anne retorted and turned on her heel.

The attorney left, and five minutes later John emerged from the bedroom, carrying a suitcase.

"I'm going to a motel until the police say I can leave town," he announced and walked out.

Marge stared at the condo door. She stared at the closed bedroom door. She turned and stared at the others in the room. "What was that about?" she asked.

"Maybe the arguing wasn't faked after all," Robert said.

Marge narrowed her eyes. "It has to be an act. To keep us from thinking they are working together."

"Maybe," said Andrew, "but the fighting is not something new. It has been going on for some time."

"Well, the hat is out in plain view now," Marge said, "And we all saw where it came from." She picked up the phone and called Detective Barker, who came out to collect the hat in one of his plastic bags after conferring with the county police.

"So, you think you solved it?" he asked.

"I'm sure of it," Marge said. "But I don't know how anyone is going to prove it. Still, as the attorney said, if there is enough doubt that Hillary did it, she won't be charged. If Hillary is off the hook, so is Robert. I guess that's all I can do."

The detective looked at her, his eyes narrowed in amusement. "Oh, no, I don't think that's all you will do. That wouldn't be the Marge Christensen I've heard so much about."

THIRTEEN

"WE'VE AGREED THAT no one wants to cook tonight," Melissa said when the detective had gone. "We're going to The Lucky Dragon for some Chinese food."

Marge was surprised when Anne decided to join them. As if sensing her feelings, Anne said, "Anything is better than sitting alone contemplating the end of my marriage. Even going out with people who have decided I'm a murderer. Now, I am ready for a good stiff drink, or two or three, and all we have in this place is wine and beer."

After they were seated at the restaurant, it seemed that several of them were ready for two or three stiff drinks. Since Marge had already had a glass of wine at the condo, she nursed the first one and watched the activity around the table. Richard and Robert both hovered around Hillary, who seemed alternately pleased and uneasy with the attention. She drank from her gin and tonic as if she were thirsty. Melissa, also sipping slowly at her wine, was trying to interest Anne in sampling the Chinese tea, but Anne brushed her aside and ordered another scotch. Andrew called the server over to get some food on the table as quickly as possible.

"Hey," Anne said, looking happier now that she was well oiled. "I like your daughter. She's a good listener. I bet she'd be a good friend. Wonder how she got you for a mother?"

Marge ignored the barb. "She said she likes you, too. Do you plan to stay in touch?"

Anne shrugged. "Who knows what I'll do after I divorce that jerk. See if he can make it on his own—he's been living off me long enough. And with Craig gone, who knows how the brass will decide to handle our department. Do you?" She turned to Andrew.

"Not a word to me so far," Andrew said. "I have a feeling they're waiting to be sure none of us is indicted for Craig's murder before they move on."

"Yeah," Anne said. "Like you all tried to blame me. Well, let me tell you something. Craig had his faults, and he wasn't afraid to manipulate people to get what he wanted, but he was a go-getter. He may have run around on his wife, but at least he supported her financially."

Hillary's head jerked up. "What little you know," she said, with more force in her voice than Marge had ever heard. "He doled out the nickels and dimes as long as I played his game—never enough to feel comfortable though. But, he did let you get away with the story that he raped you, didn't he? So, of course you would take his side."

Oh, my, Marge thought. Maybe I should have gotten them drunk a long time ago. Melissa was looking at her with raised eyebrows, as if the same thought was going through her mind.

"What story?" Anne asked. Her voice had suddenly

dropped a notch, and she looked at Andrew with what appeared to be worry in her eyes. Could she be concerned about what he believed? Would he have something to say about her future with the company? "It happened."

"Maybe once," Hillary said. "What about all the other times, even after he started seeing Carmella?"

"He made me?" Anne asked, as if hoping to be believed. Wasn't she sure about that, Marge wondered. "He would have told John and the execs. My life would have been finished." Her voice was now barely above a whisper.

Hillary snorted. "As if you cared about John. And the execs would do whatever Craig wanted them to, you should know that. You think he limited his little games to his coworkers? How do you think he kept his job?"

Tears stood in Anne's eyes. "He wasn't that bad. You had to know how he grew up. How he had to struggle and fight to get out from under the legacy of his alcoholic parents."

Movement around the table stopped. All eyes were on Anne.

"You think I didn't know?" Hillary asked. "He rubbed it in my face every day, how I grew up such a useless little princess with parents who catered to my every whim while he had to go out and fight the world. And how I should be happy he was willing to keep coddling me, even though I wasn't worth it."

Anne stared at Hillary for a long time, tears running down her cheeks. After another glance at Andrew, she heaved a sigh as if coming to a decision. "I don't know why he stayed with you. You were nothing to him. Neither was Carmella. We would have been so good together, we could have set the world on fire." She turned to Marge. "I don't know how you could even think I might kill him. I loved him. I had to hide it or he would never have seen me again. And after he was killed I thought . . . I don't know what I thought. I wanted to protect myself and even John from suspicion, so I didn't say anything. John has been out of work for six months now. He knew our marriage was on the rocks. He didn't need to be thrown to the wolves over Craig on top of that."

So would John help Anne murder the man she loved? Not likely. Nor could Marge see Anne helping John murder the man who may have ruined his marriage. John could have cared for Anne enough to murder her rapist, but it didn't look as though Anne had been raped. And Anne's love, spurned, could have driven her to murder—but not together. They didn't have a reason to do it together.

Marge shook her head. As drunk as Anne was, Marge was sure she was telling the truth. Especially since talking so openly in front of Andrew and Richard could mark the end of her job. So, marriage difficulties and unemployment were what was on John's mind. And he probably felt worse than Anne could recognize that she was supporting him. It was certainly enough to explain his glum look and stand-offish behavior all week. Marge wondered how much of this Anne had told Kate Saturday night.

Still, nothing had changed as far as the police were concerned, unless Anne had reason to repeat this story to them. Since Marge didn't think she had convinced the police Anne and John might have killed Craig, they weren't likely to question Anne again. Hillary's attorney should have no trouble making his case that several people had as much motive and opportunity as Hillary and could have contrived the evidence. That was all that was needed to get Hillary off. Even if the police did decide to go after Anne and John, their attorney should be able to make the same case, so Marge didn't have to feel guilty if she had instigated that action. And if Hillary was in the clear, Marge was sure Robert would also be in the clear. After that, she reminded herself, it was no concern of hers.

Except for the irresistible itch to find the truth.

Food arrived and they all tried to get past the tensions of the moment in order to eat. They ended up taking most of it home in carryout boxes.

"We really needed this," Melissa said as she stashed the leftovers in the refrigerator, "More food. You realize tomorrow is our last full day here? We have to check out by noon on Friday. Are you planning on going home if this still isn't solved?"

"We can get a motel room," Robert said. "Please say you'll stay, Mom."

Marge sank into a chair. "I don't know. I don't have any commitments until Monday, but I don't seem to be making any headway here. Still, I hate to leave with everything up in the air. Something is niggling at me and I can't figure out what it is."

"Relax and it will come to you," Melissa said. "Now that we are safely at home and no longer responsible for any heavy drinkers, would you like another glass of wine? I know we've already had two, but it's been a long and stressful evening."

"I would," Marge said, and accepted it gratefully. "And maybe we can heat up that Cashew Chicken. I'm suddenly hungry."

The phone rang while Melissa was working in the kitchen. She picked it up, listened, and handed it to Marge. "Kate," she mouthed.

"How's it going, Mom?"

"We think we might be getting somewhere," Marge said. "Did Anne seem edgy or anxious in any way when the two of you were watching the sunrise Sunday morning?"

The line was silent for a moment. "No," Kate said. "We talked a lot. I like her."

She paused before deciding to let Kate know what they had been thinking before they went out to dinner.

"You've got to be kidding," Kate said. "That's a lot of supposition."

"Yes, we know," Marge said. "Everything we come up with is filled with a lot of supposition. Anyway, we've pretty much talked ourselves out of it being Anne and John after Hillary and Anne's outbursts tonight." She had to stop and explain to Kate about the scene at the restaurant.

"Anne told me she and John were having problems," Kate said. "That's why they were bickering all evening, and why John didn't want to join Anne for the sunrise. John has been moping around for the six months he's been out of work, and Anne is fed up with that and his not being aggressive about looking for a job. I don't think they could work together on anything right now."

"You're sure she wasn't feeding you a line?" Marge asked.

"I'm sure. The tone of their disagreements all evening and Anne's letting out of her pent-up feelings with me were totally sincere."

"I would say that puts us back to square one," Marge said.

"Maybe not quite," Kate said. "Everyone either seems to have an alibi or doesn't have a strong enough reason to kill Craig, so I don't think you should stop looking for a stronger reason than any you have found so far, if you don't count Hillary's. But you may have something in the idea of two people working together and setting up alibis for each other, like you thought Anne and John did."

"Okay, thanks for the fresh perspective. I can see why you're the lawyer in the family. Did you know Robert stayed here, at the request of the police?"

"Nooo . . . How is it going between Hillary and him?"

Marge heard a note of caution in Kate's voice, so she knew she wasn't the only one worried about it. She glanced up at Robert, who was having a conversation with Melissa on the other side of the room. Hoping he wouldn't overhear, she told Kate about Robert spending yesterday with Hillary. When she added that Hillary and Richard had taken off together today, Kate said, "Good. He needs to get off that knight-in-shining-armor kick before he gets too involved with her. There's something about her little helpless act that I don't like, even if she was in an abusive relationship."

Marge's head jerked up. "Robert said she wasn't like that before the marriage."

"I'm not sure I would trust Robert's judgment when it comes to women."

Marge had to strangle a laugh. It was too true to be funny.

Melissa had the chicken ready by the time Marge got off the phone. After a few bites, Marge started playing with her food. "Kate suggested we might be right that two people could have planned this together, even if it wasn't John and Anne. It would explain why everyone seems to have alibis for at least one of the two events: the murder and the car running us down. To tell the truth, I'm also having a hard time believing anyone would kill for any of the reasons we've come up with so far." Except, she thought, Hillary. As much as she tried to get away from it, she kept coming back to Hillary. Even without the added complication of her daughter, women in abusive relationships have been known to kill their husbands.

"If Carmella were one of the two people, she could have given someone else the keys to her car. Her accomplice could have been the one driving it while she was busy with the police. The other person would have to be someone at the Point Brown Condo because the gun was evidently taken from Craig and Hillary's room and it ended up back there. Also, if we are sure it wasn't Anne, someone had to plant the hat in Anne's room and Anne's hairs on the pink sweat suit.

And that scenario would give Carmella a better reason than she claimed for hanging around after her encounter with Craig."

The niggling suspicion that she was missing something she should be seeing grew again in Marge's mind.

"Let's take another look at Saturday night," she said. "According to the statements, Carmella was at the motel. Everyone else returned about three-thirty in the morning except Andrew and me, who retired early. Craig went out to see Carmella. As far as we know, everyone stayed in except for Kate and Anne, who were together until seven-thirty or so, when they both were observed returning to their condos. Did Hillary say exactly what time Craig left?"

"Not that I can recall," Robert said. "We got back around three-thirty, so he must have left soon after that."

Marge jotted that down as a question to ask.

"Carmella said they were at the motel and had a huge fight which the neighbors would testify to. I wonder if the police checked out exactly what the neighbors did hear, and at what time." She shook her head. "Not having all the information makes it hard. And I doubt that we can ask Carmella any more questions without a good reason."

She wrote down the second question.

"I wonder if they've gone to bed over there," mused Marge.

"Even if they haven't," Melissa said, "they were pretty far out of it by the time we left the restaurant."

Marge grinned. "But we got more information out of Anne when she was drunk than we ever did before. And Hillary, too, for that matter. Do you suppose they kept drinking after they got home?"

"I sincerely hope not," Melissa said. "I wouldn't want to face their tomorrow if they did."

"Let me call and see if Hillary can tell me what time

Craig left," Robert said. "I'd like to be sure she got home okay, anyway."

Without waiting for approval, he went to the phone and called. When he hung up, he said, "They got back at three-thirty, as we knew, and he left immediately after that. He told her to go to bed; he wanted to walk on the beach for a while. So, that means she called me right after he left."

"Well," Marge said, "I guess we should wait for morning to see if Detective Barker knows what the neighbors heard of the altercation between Carmella and Craig—if he'll tell us."

On Thursday morning the telephone pulled Marge like a magnet, creating a nearly irresistible urge to pick it up and call Detective Barker long before he was likely to be at work. After checking her watch for at least the fiftieth time, she couldn't wait any longer and dialed the station number. Marge was surprised to be put straight through to him.

"Do you know what Carmella's neighbors heard and at what time?" she asked without preamble.

"Yes," he answered.

Marge couldn't think of any way to wheedle the information out of him, so she asked directly, "Would you be able to share that with me?"

"Why?"

"Because if the neighbors corroborate Carmella's story about the fight, it validates what she told us and makes her less likely a suspect."

"Wait a minute. Weren't you convinced last night that Anne and John Jacobs did it? What's this now about Carmella LaCosta?"

"Detective Barker, you know the county police are building a case against Hillary and not looking at other possibilities. I don't want to make the same mistake. I want to make sure to cover all the bases."

"I think you'll find they are looking at other people, too."

Marge waited, holding her breath, but he didn't elaborate and she knew he wouldn't tell her who else might be suspect.

"Okay," he said finally, "if it will get you off this kick. The neighbors did hear something—a woman shouting and loud noises like things being thrown about."

"Only a woman's voice?" Marge asked.

A pause. "You are quick. Yes, only a woman's voice."

"So, there isn't any proof Craig ever reached her condo?"

Another silence. Marge broke it this time. "And what time was this?"

"About five-thirty in the morning."

Marge sat up. "Five-thirty? Carmella told us that Craig left between five and five-thirty. Did the police compare the times?"

"I'm sure they did good police work," Detective Barker said. "And she may have remembered the time wrong. At any rate, this conversation is finished. I think I'm sorry I told you anything."

Marge hung up and turned to Robert and Melissa. "I wonder if Craig was at Carmella's at all. What if they arranged for him to come over, but Carmella lay in wait and killed him when he was on his way. She then hightailed it back to her room and staged the fight at five-thirty, either using the TV or some pre-recorded noise to simulate a fight. But, we never came up with a convincing reason why Carmella would kill Craig. Because he lied to her? Because he wouldn't marry her? Those are pretty weak motives, especially since Andrew says she was more conniving than passionate. And we know she didn't love him. Besides, how would she get the gun? She would need an inside accomplice. We're still missing something. Let's see if we can get the Point Brown group together and hash out everything we know one more time."

A phone call confirmed everyone in the Point Brown group was still at the condo. While they had not all emerged from their bedrooms yet, Andrew told Marge that Melissa, Robert, and Marge could join them.

"Still nosing around where you don't belong?" Anne asked as they were trooped into the condo's warmth, which was welcome after the walk over.

"Anne, that's not fair," Hillary said. "They are trying to help me."

Robert went to her side and she looked up at him with gratitude. "Thank you, Robert, for getting your mother to help me. If anyone can get me out of this, I have a feeling she can."

Robert took her hand and held it between his two. Marge looked around for Richard, hoping he was still in competition for taking care of Hillary.

They heard the door to the condo open; a moment later John appeared at the top of the stairs. "Richard has offered to drive you home," he said to Anne. "If you'll return the rental car, I'll be out of the apartment before you arrive."

"I thought you went to a motel last night," Marge blurted.

"I did. But now I've cleared my leaving with the police and made sure Anne has a ride home so I don't have to pay for a one-way rental car." He left before any more questions could delay him, banging the door as he went.

"That was thoughtful," Melissa said, glancing at Marge. Marge shook her head to clear it. The John she had thought killed Craig for seducing his wife would either also hate his wife or be so in love with her he couldn't leave her. This John seemed thoughtful and concerned, but definitely didn't have any problem leaving.

Richard emerged from his room and went to Hillary. "How are you this morning?" he asked. Hillary smiled up at him with the same grateful look she had bestowed on Robert a moment before. Marge studied Richard closely. A few days ago all his attention had been on Kate. Had that been a cover for his interest in Hillary? If John didn't kill Craig over his involvement with Anne, had Richard killed Craig to get to Hillary?

Richard left Hillary's side and went to Anne. "Are you okay?" he asked. His concern appeared as deep and genuine as it had with Hillary, his look no less intense. Marge frowned before a slow smile spread across her face. There were people in the world, after all, who had genuine concern for other people's feelings.

Why in the world wasn't this man married? Or did the caring trait emphasize his feminine side?

Andrew announced coffee was ready and Anne helped him pass out steaming mugs to everyone.

Hillary looked up at Andrew when he handed her a mug. "I sure hope you aren't planning on going back to Carmella," she said, her voice low but hard.

Andrew's head jerked up. "Why would I do that?" he asked. "She left me, remember? I'm not a glutton for punishment."

"I always wondered how devastated you were when she left you for Craig," Hillary said.

Now Marge's head snapped up. Was this the same Hillary who Andrew had called a little mouse that couldn't hurt anyone? Even Robert looked a little shaken.

Hillary seemed to sense the reaction to her remark and immediately looked sad and contrite. "Forgive me. I'm not myself this morning."

Andrew beckoned Marge into the kitchen while the others remained in the living area.

"Remember the day you came and I was the only one here? And you caught me staring out the window?"

"Yes," Marge said, "while the police were talking with Hillary."

"I didn't tell you what I saw because it didn't make any sense. A woman in a yellow sweat suit, which made me think of Carmella for some reason, seemed to be keeping an eye on the condo. She had her head covered and her face down so I couldn't be sure who it was." He grinned. "It was a yellow sweat suit—if it had been a pink one I would have spoken sooner."

"What would Carmella be doing down here, especially after Craig was killed?"

"That's why I didn't say anything. I'm still not sure it was her, but I thought I should mention it. The gun had already been discovered and she couldn't get into the condo to plant the hat—so what would she have been doing here?"

"Maybe she needed to touch base with her accomplice, or make sure said accomplice had retrieved the hat and the gun," Marge said.

Andrew looked at Marge. "Her what?"

"Carmella could have left the gun and the hat somewhere outside earlier, and an accomplice inside the condo picked them up and put the gun in Hillary's room and planted the hat in Anne's."

Andrew frowned. "Why would they do that? If they hid the gun somewhere else, it would be more likely to implicate Hillary."

"Maybe they didn't want to implicate Hillary. They wanted it to look like a plant. And mostly they wanted to muddy the waters. So much of what we know doesn't make sense that it could have been done only to confuse the investigation."

"Look like a plant?"

Marge closed her eyes. Of course, *look* like a plant. Yes, all the evidence indicated two people worked to murder Craig in such a way that neither of them could be accused. Her mistake was thinking those two people had to be John and Anne. If not for Kate's statement, she would probably not have been open to see the other possibilities.

"Marge, are you okay?" Andrew asked.

She was staring across at Robert and Hillary huddled together. This was not a path she wanted to follow. But, she was Robert's mother. She was bound to believe he was innocent, wasn't she?

FOURTEEN

MARGE SWUNG AROUND and headed for the door. Andrew hesitated a moment before following. "Let's go for a walk," she said, beckoning to Melissa to join them. Right or wrong, she was going to follow the other paths. She was going to ignore the closeness of Robert and Hillary. She was going to forget how many times Robert had been in the Point Brown condo; opportunities when he could have planted evidence or helped someone inside the condo do it. She was going to ignore Robert's protective instincts, which she couldn't even begin to believe would lead him to commit murder.

"Andrew, tell me about the times you saw Hillary and Carmella together," she said when they reached the parking lot.

When his brow went up, Marge thought he was going to ask why. Instead, his expression changed from surprise to conjecture as he seemed to be searching his memory.

"Well, I know I saw them at a couple of office functions. How Craig got away with having them both there is a matter for the executives to decipher. Carmella seemed to revel in opportunities to snub Hillary. Hillary ostentatiously avoided her, seeking sympathy from whoever was around." He frowned. "Now that I think about it, Hillary seemed to make sure whoever she was near noticed Carmella's actions. Like she wanted to be sure everyone knew how badly Craig treated her."

"And, you never saw them together any other time?"

Andrew looked at her, frowning. "Why would they be together unless Craig arranged it?" The frown deepened.

"What?"

"At one TGIF gathering, Craig acted surprised when Carmella arrived; he didn't seem pleased. He grabbed her and steered her away from the group. The reason I remember is because, when I turned to see how Hillary was taking it, I caught a smug smile for a moment before she adopted her put-upon look."

"Andrew, why didn't you mention this before?"

Andrew shook his head. "You have a way of jarring the memory, Marge. I honestly had forgotten that incident until just this minute. But surely it doesn't change anything. I figured Hillary was happy that Carmella had angered Craig. A little bit of revenge, maybe."

"But everyone keeps telling me Hillary didn't care about Craig's affairs. She only seemed to object to them to get pity from people. Why would she suddenly care that he appeared to be angry with Carmella?" Marge shook her head. "I was sure that Anne or John killed Craig, but it seemed impossible unless they did it together. Now we know they weren't apt to act together, but it still probably needed two people to make it work. Either two people from your group lured Carmella here to make her a suspect, or Carmella is working with one person in your group. If so, who could that person be?" Marge held her breath while she waited for Andrew's answer. She prayed he wouldn't think of the only other person outside their group who might have been involved.

It appeared he was more concerned about who the "inside" one might be. He threw up his hands. "I promise you, Marge, I did not kill Craig, sneak back in, and later join you to go to church." He stopped and gripped Marge's arm, spinning her around to face him. "Tell me you don't truly believe I am capable of helping to kill Craig and then working with you to try and find his killer."

Marge dropped her eyes. That wasn't what she thought happened, but how could she be sure? Jumping into the opening Andrew had given her, she said, "That would be one way to always know what was happening."

Andrew's fingers dug into her arm for another moment before he dropped it and strode back into the condo. Marge rubbed the bruised area and stared after him.

Melissa had been standing back watching the exchange. "Marge, think," she said. "If Andrew were working with Carmella, why would he have told you he saw her lurking outside the condos? Besides, everything you said could also apply to Richard."

"I know." Marge choked back the tears that threatened. "I don't think either of them did it, and Andrew didn't deserve that. What is the matter with me?"

"Maybe I can help you there," Melissa said. Marge winced when Melissa touched her bruised arm and guided her towards the road back to Mariner Village. "All mixed up in the murder investigation is your conflict over developing a relationship with a man. Pete's arrival put that conflict front and center, and you took it out on Andrew."

Marge stared at Melissa. Could that have a bearing on her actions? "And, if you're right? What do I do now? How can I ever apologize?"

"I don't know. I guess if I were you I'd let it go for now, let him cool off while you get this murder solved, and think about it later with a clearer head."

Laughter bubbled up through the tears. "Are you so sure I can solve this murder? And that I have a clear head?"

"I have no doubt whatsoever, to either," Melissa said, her voice firm. A few minutes later, she added, "So, if neither Richard nor Andrew is the "inside" partner, and you've ruled out Anne and John, that only leaves Hillary. We've known all along Hillary had the strongest motive, but everyone has been convinced she was incapable of murder."

Marge let the silence linger before she answered. "If Carmella is involved, she is probably the one who actually killed Craig. The inside person would do the planting of evidence and muddying of the waters."

"Do you think Hillary might be capable of doing that, knowing she was helping murder Craig?"

The phone was ringing when they walked into the condo. Marge rushed to answer it.

"Marge?"

"Diane? What's wrong? Is it Mom?"

"Yes, it's your mother. She's driving me nuts. When are you going to come home and help me out?"

"I don't know, Diane. I'll have to see when I can get time and money to make the trip. Has something happened?"

"Ha! You have time and money enough to take a vacation at the ocean but not to help take care of your mother. Typical." The phone slammed in Marge's ear.

"No!" Marge cried, staring at the receiver. "I can't deal with this now."

"What?" Melissa asked.

Marge explained the call and the reason for it. "She never told me if Mom is okay. All she said was that she's driving her nuts. The problem is I can't trust my sister to separate irritation at being inconvenienced from a real issue."

"Is there someone you can call? Someone who is objective enough to tell you the real situation?"

Marge thought for a moment. "Yes, my Aunt Valerie spends her summers in Traverse City. She always seems to be able to see right to the heart of whatever is going on."

"Well, call her. Get it off your mind so you can go back to what's going on here."

Marge dialed. A busy tone buzzed in her ear. "I'll have to try to forget about that for now," she said.

Unable to sit still, Marge paced, arms hugged across her stomach. Pink sweat suits. But pink didn't fit either Carmella or Anne. Carmella in a yellow sweat suit, lurking round the Point Brown condos. Hillary's pink sweat suit with Anne's red hair on it. But Anne had an alibi for the time of the murder; she couldn't have worn it then, so what difference did it make if she borrowed it some other time? And why would she? The only other way the hair could have gotten on the collar was if someone in the condo had put it there.

It had always seemed strange that Craig brought his gun to the beach. Did he? Or did Hillary? No one thought Hillary would be able to kill someone, but could she have brought the gun for someone else to do it, placed the gun where the other person could find it, and retrieved the gun after Craig was shot with it?

Marge remembered a movie where the wife and the mistress killed the husband. Was it for his life insurance? Would the wife share it with the mistress? Or was the motive to get rid of a cheating spouse, especially if he had already cheated on the mistress? Or to get an overbearing bully out of their lives? For Marge, that would be the best motive.

She froze. Would she murder in those circumstances? She was sure she could never take a life; thank God she would never have to find out.

Frowning and shaking her head, she dialed Detective Barker's number. "Please don't be upset with me," she said. "I need to know, do the county police think Hillary might have killed Craig for his life insurance?"

After a lengthy pause, Detective Barker answered. "As a matter of fact, they did. But they discovered Craig Carlson had no life insurance except a small policy through his company. Strange for a man who sold life insurance, isn't it? Evidently he didn't care what happened to his wife if he died. But—you never told me what happened to your suspicion of the Jacobs? Not long ago you were certain they were the ones who worked together to kill him."

"I know. I feel guilty about judging them so quickly. It turns out the way they were behaving probably had to do with their own relationship, not with Craig's involvement with Anne."

"You're on to something, Marge Christensen," Melissa said when Marge hung up the phone and stood staring at it for a while. Marge shook her head again. She could no longer deny the direction her thoughts were taking her.

"Wait," she replied. "We'll see."

Pulling out her sketchpad and water color pencils, she sat at the dining room table and bent to the task. Robert walked in while she was working.

"Shh," Melissa said, beckoning him into the living room. "Her fingers are remembering something."

Marge quickly sketched in a minimal background for the holiday bazaar. With more detail, she added Craig to the scene, the surprise and anger on his face when he spotted Carmella, and Carmella's look of narrow-eyed triumph at upsetting him. She roughed in the men in the back corner, talking; noted the concern on Robert's distracted face as he looked at Hillary. Hillary, Kate, and Anne were scattered around the room browsing. Except Hillary wasn't going through the merchandise. She had her hands resting on a child's outfit while she was looking in the same direction as Craig. Her expression was not surprise. It was not anger. Marge stared at the sketch, not willing to believe what her fingers had told her.

"Can this be?" she whispered.

"Can what be?" Melissa asked, reaching out.

Marge pulled the sketch back, out of Melissa's vision. She hugged it close to her chest. If she showed Melissa the sketch, she would be opening a new can of worms and she didn't know if she dared to do that. And yet . . . her fingers had never lied. Melissa reached over and pried Marge's hands away from the pad.

"It didn't register until I drew it, but I know this is what I saw," Marge said, her voice low and tight. "What do you see?"

"Are you thinking what I think you are?" Melissa asked.

"Yes, I believe I am. But it's not an accusation I can make unless I'm sure. And unless I can figure out how it affects the whole picture."

"True. Even if we're right, it doesn't mean either of them had anything to do with killing Craig. Hillary might have been reacting with pleasure to the fact that Carmella irritated Craig again."

Marge studied the sketch. "I don't think so. That's not what I see in Hillary's eyes. I see something closer to adoration. She's had bad relationships with two men, and she is a dependent person. At the very least, she appears to be looking at her rescuer."

"What?" Robert jumped up from the loveseat and grabbed the sketch. "What are you talking about?"

Marge and Melissa were silent while he studied the sketch. "You're reading too much into this," he said. "It's impossible. Hillary came to me. She . . . she came to *me*."

Marge closed her eyes. Her fear had been well founded. Even Hillary ignoring him yesterday hadn't convinced Robert that Hillary wasn't relying on him to rescue her. How could he possibly accept what Marge saw in the picture?

Melissa studied the drawing some more. "Robert, I'm afraid your mother is right. You might be one of the things Carmella and Hillary were using to muddy the waters." She turned to Marge. "Do you think it *was* more than a rescue and Craig found out?"

Marge shrugged, feeling helpless. "I believe it was more. And it was a constant threat that he would find out, even if he hadn't yet."

"Well, so what?" Melissa said. "Hillary wouldn't be the first woman to find solace with another woman after having bad heterosexual relationships. Nor would she be the first to discover what made her truly happy only after it had been offered to her." Melissa paused. "So, why didn't she leave Craig?"

Robert stared at the two of them, disbelief written all over his face. "How can you say something like that based on a drawing? How do you know you didn't just dream up that look because of what you were already thinking?"

Marge went to Robert, aching to comfort him, but he shrank away. "Robert, everyone else has been ruled out. It almost had to be two people, either Hillary and Carmella or Hillary and . . ."

Both Robert and Melissa stared at Marge.

"You suspected me?" Robert's voice was hoarse.

"No, Robert, no, but the police might have. Why do you think they showed so much interest in you?"

"You suspected me," Robert whispered and sank down on the loveseat with his head in his hands.

Marge held out her hands in a helpless gesture. Would he ever believe she never seriously thought he was a murderer? Would he ever forgive her if he didn't?

Dropping her hands, she turned away. She couldn't dwell on that now. All her attention had to be directed at finding out if she was right about who the real killer was before the police followed the same line of thinking she had, but without the advantage of the painting, and came after Robert.

She turned to answer Melissa. "She couldn't leave him," she said. She nearly bit her tongue. Melissa flicked a questioning look at her, and Marge longed to spill it all out and get Melissa's reactions, but she had promised to keep Hillary's secret. No matter what Hillary had done, Marge had to honor her promise.

Or did she? Did she have to honor the promise if it meant letting Hillary get away with murder? Marge felt herself go still, her breathing shallow. She shook her head. "No," she finally managed to say, "somehow we have to figure this out without delving into why she couldn't leave him. I can't risk a promise I made to Hillary."

"But . . ."

Marge raised her hands, cutting off whatever Melissa was about to say. "I'm sorry, I really can't say any more. We are now pretty sure Carmella has a strong enough motive, and she can't prove her whereabouts at the time of Craig's murder." She stopped, frowning. "But *does* Carmella have the same motive as Hillary? You've given a pretty good reason why Hillary might turn to a woman, but who could ever imagine Carmella is gay?"

Melissa shrugged. "How does a gay person look different? Or act different? They come in all varieties, the same as the rest of us. It appears Carmella did whatever she had to do to get ahead. Maybe that same helpless quality in Hillary that has all the men taking care of her touched Carmella's heart and persuaded her to come out."

Gazing at Melissa, Marge's thoughts were in turmoil. "At this point, given their different personalities, I'd guess Carmella's the one who killed Craig. Hillary must have brought the gun, involved Robert in order to throw off suspicion, and planted evidence to implicate Anne."

"No," Robert said, but his voice lacked conviction. "Not Hillary. She couldn't do anything like that."

"Not by herself. But she could have helped Carmella," said Marge.

Melissa stared at her. "So, what do we do now?"

"We may not need to do anything. I don't think the police can charge Hillary or Carmella on the evidence they have right now. And, if they can't, we can forget about it. If they can, we probably should tell them what we suspect."

Melissa narrowed her eyes. "So, you would let them get away with it to protect Robert's feelings?"

Marge shook her head, but she wished Melissa hadn't so quickly seen through her. "We don't have proof of any of this," she said. "And everybody claims Hillary couldn't hurt a fly. She was too cowed by Craig to do anything; can you really see her helping to murder him? Remember what the attorney said. We don't have to prove guilt or innocence. We only have to create doubt."

"Thank you, Mom," Robert said. "I know you're wrong about Hillary and Carmella. You have to be."

Melissa wasn't so easy. "In other words, you're going to help the killers muddy the waters some more. You're going to do what you keep accusing the police of doing. You're going to try to find facts that fit what you want to believe and ignore everything else."

Marge dropped her head into her hands. "I only promised Robert I'd help Hillary. I don't have to muddy any waters or find any facts at this point. It's up to the police to solve the murder."

Melissa stood and walked to the slider. "What about your sketch? What about the truth you always say is so important? Can you pretend your fingers didn't remember seeing what they saw?"

Pacing around the room, Marge glanced at Robert. He was watching her with a hopeful look in his eyes. Did she owe it to Robert to look after Hillary anymore? And if she did, and if Hillary got away with murder, then what? Did Marge want to risk the possibility that Hillary's dalliance with Carmella was a pretense; that Hillary would drop the pretense once she didn't need Carmella anymore; that Hillary would after all attach herself to Robert, her knight in shining armor?

Actually, her decision couldn't be made based on any of that. What was between Hillary and Carmella or even Robert had no bearing on the actions she should take. She stopped and took a deep breath. Whether Robert understood or not, she had to do what she knew was right.

"You're right, of course," she finally said.

"Mom, no . . ."

"I'm sorry, Robert. If we're correct, Hillary is an accessory to murder and I don't want her to be a part of your life. If we're wrong, you and Hillary both deserve to have that proven so it doesn't hang over your heads. Only then can you decide if you have a future together. We have to go ahead with this. But I don't know how we're going to prove what happened." She returned to pacing. "Given that Hillary was in the condo, and called Robert to prove it, we can assume Carmella was the killer. How could they have worked it out together?"

Melissa poured two mugs of coffee, handed one to Marge, and sat back on the sofa with an expectant grin crinkling the corners of her blue eyes. "Think out loud, please," she said.

"Okay. Carmella would have to get the gun. Could they risk being seen if Hillary gave it to Carmella in Bellevue before coming to Ocean Shores?" Marge stopped pacing and caught her breath.

"What?" Robert and Melissa chorused.

"Hillary left her purse on a table a couple aisles over from where we all were at the bazaar. Anne discovered it and returned it to her. Hillary looked inside the purse, as anyone would in that situation. I assumed she satisfied herself that nothing was missing. But what if she was really making sure that something had been taken out—like a gun?" She stopped and thought a minute. "Sometime before the group left Aberdeen, could Hillary have called Carmella to let her know we were on our way, so they could time their actions?"

Both women looked at Robert, whose brow furrowed, as if reluctant to take part in the thinking process. He finally spoke. "She went to the ladies' room by herself while the rest of us were walking out of the bar. She was alone, and could have called Carmella on her cell phone."

Marge nodded and continued. "When Craig left the condo to go to Carmella's motel, Hillary calls Carmella again." She stopped, looked at Robert, and frowned. "And she called Robert. Why?"

The pain in Robert's eyes almost made Marge stop. "She wanted me to come to Mariner Village after Craig left. She said she needed someone to be with her." Marge thought he might begin to cry when he continued. "I can't believe I said I was too tired to go. I reminded her that both Richard and Andrew were there. But, if I had gone, if I had been there with her, you would know she didn't have anything to do with Craig's murder."

"But," Marge said, "what if she really wanted to get you out of the condo at the same time as Craig so suspicion would fall on you? Maybe that is why she convinced you to come to Ocean Shores in the first place."

She returned to her line of reasoning. "By now Carmella could already be on the embankment above the driftwood where Craig was found, because she wouldn't have time to get there if she had waited for Hillary's phone call. That's why the dune grass was crushed in that area." She looked over to see Melissa busily taking notes. "What are you doing?" she asked.

"Making sure I get this all down so we don't forget anything when we tell the police," she said.

Marge smiled. "Good thinking. Anyway, when Craig comes by, Carmella lures him over somehow. She waits until he is right below her, behind the driftwood, and she shoots. But why wouldn't someone hear the gunshot?"

"She could have muffled it somehow," Robert suggested, his voice sounding strangled. "The noise from the surf and the rain might have helped. Plus everyone was sound asleep by then."

Marge looked at Robert, surprised he was contributing. He wouldn't have any problem if Carmella were guilty but could he still believe someone other than Hillary gave her the gun?

"Anyway," she continued, "Carmella returns to her motel room and stages the fight, maybe playing something that she recorded earlier, to make it appear Craig is with her. Sometime on Sunday, she jogs over to Point Brown, wearing a pink sweat suit in case anyone should see her, and stashes the gun, wiped clean of prints, in a prearranged place. Hillary picks up the gun when everyone is out searching for Craig and plants it in her own room."

Marge paused to think a minute. "If the pink hat is not Hillary's, either she and Carmella bought matching hats or Carmella also passed the hat on to Hillary to plant in Anne's room and further complicate matters."

She picked up her now lukewarm coffee and took a sip. "Carmella hangs around to see how things are going. Maybe she gave Hillary a key to her car, and they agree that if Carmella is taken in for questioning, Hillary will do something with the car to draw suspicion away from Carmella."

Marge took a huge gulp of coffee and stared at Melissa. She hardly dared look at Robert. "This is starting to make sense," she said. "Actually, this makes more sense than anything else we have considered."

Robert's shoulders sagged and his head hung in a way Marge hadn't seen since early in his divorce proceedings. "It can't be. There must be some other explanation." He stumbled to the door. "I'm going out for a walk. I have to think."

After the door closed behind Robert, Marge turned to Melissa. "When I get back to Bellevue, I am going to search until I find a good woman for Robert."

Melissa laughed. "What makes you think you and he would agree on who is a good woman?"

"Well, if he doesn't like the first one I'll find out why and try again. And again. Until we get it right. He certainly isn't doing well on his own and I'm tired of watching him get hurt."

Marge picked up the sketch and looked at it again. Even after seeing the gleam in Hillary's eyes, or maybe because of it, she had missed the look in Carmella's eyes. Carmella was gazing at Hillary with a look of pleasure; a look that was more than gloating over the beginnings of success in their plan. She was looking at someone she loved.

"I need to talk with Detective Barker," she said. "I know Lieutenant Morgan won't listen to anything I have to say based on a painting. Even Detective Barker might not listen to me again, so I have to think of something that will grab his attention. He might be interested in this sketch because Pete told him about my fingers, but it doesn't prove anything; it doesn't even give the police grounds to bring Carmella back for questioning. We need to come up with some plausible reason to question Hillary and Carmella again, together."

"What good would that do? If they stick to the stories they have given so far, they could be home free. One of them really knew how to concoct a plot."

Marge thought a moment, studying the picture. "What do you think Hillary would do if she thought Carmella was going to be charged with murder? Or vice-versa?"

"If they truly love each other either one of them would probably confess to protect the other. But do we know if Carmella loves Hillary? Maybe she was acting out of her own agenda."

"It's possible, but the look she is giving Hillary here says otherwise. And the same could be said of Hillary. Unless, of course, either one of them is a great actress." She paced around the kitchen island. "Given their different natures, it would probably work better for Hillary to think Carmella was being charged. Hillary would be more likely to break." Unless she thought confessing would impact her daughter, Marge thought. Would she try to put all the blame on Carmella in order to protect Caitlin? "Of course, the first problem is how to convince the police to do anything at all."

FIFTEEN

"I HAVE A PLAN," MARGE said as Melissa started pulling food out of the refrigerator for lunch.

"Great. What might that be?"

"It's not a terrific plan, but it's all I can come up with. We need to have a party tonight, for our last night, and invite the Point Brown group. See if Jane can get Detective Barker to join us."

Melissa groaned. "How are we going to have a party with the leftover bits and pieces of food we have? We certainly don't want to buy more now."

"They must have leftovers at the Point Brown condo, too. We'll make it a cocktail party, pooling our leftovers to make hors d'oeuvres. We'll call it a 'clean-out-the-refrigerator' party. She eyed the array of food Melissa had selected for lunch. "Be sure you don't use anything now that could work for the party. Oh, we might have to buy a little wine or something. Remember how a couple of drinks loosened the tongues last night."

Melissa quickly took stock of what they had and selected for their lunch only those items that couldn't easily be turned into finger food. "This makes for an interesting lunch," she said with a laugh. "Don't you think you should make sure the Point Brown group can be talked into a party?"

"Right," Marge said, picking up the phone. She gulped when Andrew answered. Taking a deep breath, she said, "Andrew, I owe you an apology. I never believed you killed Craig; I was afraid my feelings were getting in the way of my judgment."

"Apology accepted," he said, but the coldness in his voice tempted Marge to hang up the phone and forget the whole thing.

"Melissa and I had a brilliant idea," she managed. Glancing up, she caught Melissa's wide-eyed, who-*me* look and nearly choked to keep from laughing. "Since this is our last night here, and we both have leftovers, why don't you bring yours over here? We can enjoy some tasty snacks made from all the bits and pieces."

"I'm not sure who here would be interested in getting together with you. You've managed to alienate every member of our group. Except maybe Richard."

Apology accepted? It didn't sound like that to Marge. She swallowed hard and pushed ahead. "I have an ulterior motive, but I can't say too much about it," Marge said. "If it works right, we may find out who killed Craig."

"Right. You've had that figured out a couple of times already, haven't you? Aren't you tired of accusing the wrong people?"

"What if the right people end up confessing?"

"How are you going to work that out?" Andrew asked.

"I can't tell you," Marge said wondering if she really could make it happen. "But it's our last chance to try to find the truth."

"Us, as opposed to the police?"

"Yes, well, I have a feeling the police are on the right track but are using the wrong tactics to get there."

"What?" Andrew almost shouted. "You mean . . . you think . . ."

"Don't say it," Marge cut in quickly, wishing she hadn't let that much out of the bag. "If anyone hears you it might ruin our chance to find out for sure."

The line was silent for a moment. "If you're thinking what I think you are, I don't believe it. However, if going along with your plan means we can clear more innocent people, I might go for it—but I know I won't be able to talk the others into going to your condo."

Marge knew by the tone of his voice that he was intrigued. "Well, if you can't come to us, we'll come to you. You decide whether you need to warn them ahead of time, but please try to make sure everyone is there."

"You know John has gone already," Andrew said.

"Yes, but that shouldn't be a problem now that we know he didn't have anything to do with the murder. Also, don't worry about preparing food ahead of time—but don't let anyone clean out the refrigerator either. We'll make the get together about creative ways to prepare good party food from leftovers. Do you have any liquor there?"

"A little beer, I think."

"Well, we'll make sure we have enough wine, too. I don't want anyone to get sloshed again, but we do need to break down the barriers a little bit. Oh, and a word of warning. I'm asking Detective Barker to join us. We need a witness who has some credibility with the county guys to verify whatever we learn so no one can deny what was said."

After a lunch of tomato soup doctored with leftover Chinese vegetables, along with salad greens—they saved the other salad makings for a plate of crudités—Marge went down to the office to invite Jane and the detective to the party.

"As it happens, I can get away on a Thursday night," Jane said. "It gets busy on Friday and Saturday, with people coming and going, so I often leave Thursday in the hands of my assistant."

"Do you think your husband will mind? It'll be sort of like a busman's holiday for him. And . . . is he working right now?"

"Yes. Why?"

"I have a huge favor to ask of him. I'll tell you about it later."

Jane laughed. "As I mentioned before, he is always ready to work. I believe he likes a good puzzle as much as you seem to."

Back in the condo, Marge called the police station.

"Detective Barker, is there any way you can get Carmella LaCosta back to Ocean Shores tonight?"

"Not legally. It's not my case, remember?"

"But you never questioned her about the car running us down, did you?"

"Hmmm. I could try, if I had a good reason. But, if she's smart enough to simply refuse, there isn't anything I can do about it. I don't have any evidence that it was her car."

"It may be easier than you think. My guess is that she's more worried about what is happening here than she lets on."

"What do you mean?"

"If I'm right, and you get her to come, you'll find out at the party tonight."

"What party?"

"You and Jane are going to join us at Point Brown for a final night party this evening."

"And you want Miss LaCosta at the party?"

"Right. You might hint that we think we figured out who killed Craig. And that's all I can say now. You have to see and hear for yourself, without me telling you what I think."

"All right, since you're so sure I won't have to do any arm twisting, I'll give it a shot. But I'm really going out on a limb this time. I hope I don't regret it."

Feeling the sun's warmth as she crossed the parking lot, Marge looked up in surprise. This had turned into the best beach day of the week. "We need to get out there," she announced to Melissa as soon as she entered the condo. "You've spent far too much of your week helping me delve into this murder instead of taking the vacation you so richly deserve."

Fifteen minutes later they were headed toward the jetty. "I believe the rocks are dry enough to safely do a little climbing," Marge said.

"No artwork today?"

The bright sun reflecting off the angles of the rocks made Marge's fingers itch to put it on paper, but this was the last chance to spend some of this week with Melissa.

Halfway to the jetty they ran into Robert on his way back to Mariner Village, his head down and his hands jammed into his pockets.

"Hey," Marge called. "What's wrong?"

He stopped and drew circles in the sand with his foot. "You were right, as usual," he said. "I went to talk to Hillary, but she made it clear that she didn't need my help anymore and she was sorry she had asked me to come. If the police don't have anything they can hold me on, I think I'll head home this afternoon."

"Stay," Marge said. "We're going to have an impromptu

party at Point Brown tonight. It might be painful for you, but I think you need to be there."

A smile chased the gloom from Robert's face, only for a moment, but enough to make Marge glad she had told him. "An impromptu party? How can it be impromptu if you already know you're going to do it?"

"Well, *we* know, but my guess is it will be a surprise for most of them."

"Mom, what are you cooking up now?"

"You'll see. Want to go rock climbing with us?"

"Aren't you a little old for rock climbing?"

"Okay, smarty, let's see who's too old." Marge took off running. Soon Melissa and Robert were racing after her.

Three hours later, sunburned and sore, they returned to the condo to get ready for the evening's adventure. Marge called Detective Barker.

"Any success?"

"Yes." He sounded puzzled. "It was surprisingly easy to convince her to come. I'm bummed that you seem to know why and won't share it with me, after all I shared with you."

Marge laughed. "Not fair, I know. But you'll see why tonight. It is important that you not know ahead of time."

After showers, they emptied the refrigerator of anything that could be used to put together snack food. "We have more than we thought," Melissa said. "I think we're going to have to take a car over."

The phone rang when they were about to leave.

"Marge?"

"Aunt Valerie! How are you?"

"I'm doing well. I imagine you called to inquire about your mother."

"Yes, Diane says Mother is getting difficult to care for and she needs my help. You know I don't have the resources

I used to have, and I need to keep my job. Can you help me figure out what to do?"

"Marge, you don't have to worry about your mother's care. Diane can well take care of her, especially after all the help your mother has given her over the years. And, Lisa is crazy about her grandmother. It wouldn't take much to get her to help."

Marge felt a weight lift from her shoulders. "Diane says Lisa doesn't pitch in. And I feel like it's my responsibility to help take care of Mother."

"You and Gene did your share when you could afford it. You helped your mother financially while she continued to help Diane. Now Diane has a good husband, who has a good business, so she doesn't need financial help. She has Lisa, who is a bit young but could be more help if Diane would give her credit. And you have to take care of yourself. You have nothing to feel guilty about.

"That being said, I think you should plan for a visit home within the next few months if you can manage it. Your mother has apparently had some small strokes. She doesn't show any physical effects except they've taken a toll on her language ability. It's impossible to predict if and when another one will happen and what it will do to her mental capabilities. You don't need to plan on staying long, but you may want a little time with her while she is still able to communicate reasonably well."

Marge felt a sinking in the pit of her stomach. "Thank you, Aunt Valerie," she managed. "I'll plan on doing that as soon as I can arrange it."

Maybe Joshua could get some students to help him at the framing shop during the Christmas holidays so she could go to Michigan. No, that wouldn't work, she couldn't be gone during her art exhibit. But she did have to go, soon. The mother who loved her sister more was still her mother, and

Marge would be devastated if she didn't get a chance to talk to her again.

Picking up a bag of food, she shook her head to clear it of those worries. They would have to wait for one more night. "Okay, let's go," she said and they left the condo for the short drive to Point Brown Resort.

"You again," Anne said when she opened the door to Marge's knock. "I think you'd know you're not welcome here."

"Speak for yourself," Andrew said, ushering them in.

Anne turned on him. "Did you know about this? Is that why you were checking to see if we were hanging around tonight?"

"Guilty," Andrew said. "But, if I understand Marge correctly, you might be glad you did."

"What's all this?" Richard asked, coming out of his room.

"This," Melissa said, "is the contents of our refrigerator. When we put it together with the contents of your refrigerator, I'll bet we can make some tasty tidbits to have with the wine we brought along."

"That sounds good," Hillary said. Her voice was guarded.

"Are you free to go home tomorrow?" Marge asked.

"Yes, of course, with the caveat that I don't leave Bellevue. Which isn't a problem. Where would I go?"

Anne pitched in, despite her initial attitude, and busied herself helping Melissa pull things out of the refrigerator and directing Richard and Robert to start matching things up and putting them together. Wine and beer all around mellowed the scene even more. By the time Detective Barker and Jane arrived with Carmella in tow, platters of tempting morsels that could have come fresh from the deli were laid out.

"Carmella," Hillary blurted, "what are you doing here?"

"I don't know," Carmella said. "This detective seemed to think I needed to come back to Ocean Shores. I thought it was for questioning or something. But," she turned and gave Detective Barker an accusing look, "to attend a party? Why?"

The detective shrugged and turned to Marge. Before Marge could say anything, Melissa stuck a glass of wine in Carmella's hand and led Jane and Detective Barker over to the refreshments.

Marge took a deep breath. It was now or never.

"So," she said, turning to Carmella, "you think you pulled one over on us, don't you?"

The room stilled. Carmella raised perfectly shaped eyebrows, a quizzical expression in her almond eyes. "What are you talking about?" she asked and popped a stuffed mushroom into her mouth.

"You killed Craig. That's why you came to Ocean Shores. You found a way to get Craig's gun, maybe before you left Bellevue, or from someone in this condo after you got here." Marge watched Carmella for a change of expression, but was disappointed. Unfortunately, she couldn't watch Hillary at the same time. "It had to be you impersonating Hillary on the beach in order to make it seem like someone was trying to frame her, or at least to confuse the issue. There was a lot of confusing the issue going on. You lured Craig out to the beach early Sunday morning, after the group returned from Aberdeen, and shot him. Later, you wiped the gun clean, and an accomplice put it in Hillary's room to confuse things even more. You didn't think Hillary could be charged. Even if she were, it would be hard to believe she would keep the gun, which made it look as if someone planted it in her room. The police would obviously think she had the best motive, but they would have no real evidence. For some reason, you hung around after the murder, probably to make sure your plan worked—or maybe to gloat at all our flailing about as we tried to discover the truth."

"Why would I do all of that? Just because Craig decided not to marry me? There are other fish in the ocean, you know." Carmella's voice was denigrating, the wave of her hand dismissive. She took a sip of wine. Marge chanced a glance at Hillary and noticed that she was making steady inroads on her wine.

Marge struggled to keep her face as impassive as Carmella's. She tried to block Hillary out of her mind and concentrate on Carmella, which allowed her to catch Carmella's quick look at Hillary. Marge turned to see the response, but Hillary looked as grief-stricken as any recent widow should. Only a flutter between her eyes, a frown coming and going, betrayed the conflict Marge hoped Hillary was feeling.

Marge made the mistake of turning toward the detective to see how he was taking it. His look of amusement almost undid her. She took a deep breath to steady herself and turned back to Carmella.

"Why did you get your accomplice to pretend to run us down with your car when the police had you in for questioning? Why would you risk the car being traced to you?"

Something made Marge pause. Was that a tiny crack she saw in Carmella's calm exterior? Did that mean the running her down with the car wasn't Carmella's idea? Maybe it was Hillary's, and Hillary had done it without Carmella's permission. Why?

Whatever it was, Carmella recovered quickly. Cocking her head, defiance in her eyes, she smiled a closed mouth smile that said she wasn't at all worried.

Marge took a deep breath to calm the churning in her stomach. What had given her the idea this storybook ploy would work in real life? She should have known Carmella was too smart to give anything away. Carmella had to know it was her neck on the line because she was the one who had pulled the trigger. If Marge proved that the two of them did it and Hillary played her cards right, Hillary might get off with a slap on the wrist while Carmella went to prison. Was Carmella so in love with Hillary she was willing to do that? Had Marge chosen the wrong person to grill?

She had to change her tactics. Throwing an apologetic look at Robert, she turned to Hillary. With her voice as soft and gentle as she could make it, she asked, "How do you think Carmella got the gun, Hillary?"

Hillary's dark-blue eyes were as round and deep as the ocean.

"How could she get it into your room?"

Marge thought she detected a ripple of fear, quickly squelched.

"I don't know anything about the gun. Craig must have brought it to the shore. He must have had it with him that night. Someone must have taken it away from him and shot him. I don't know how it got back into my room." Hillary's voice was almost a whisper. She looked up. With a little more force, she added, "Everyone has been in and out all the time, including Robert and you."

Marge blinked. "When have I ever been in this condo alone?"

"Robert was."

Marge swallowed hard to keep her expression noncommittal. She turned to Robert. "Really? Alone?"

Robert's eyes were wide with betrayal. Marge had to turn away from the pain she saw in them. "For about two minutes," he said. "Because Hillary went out to get something she had left in the car."

"Well, that won't fly," Marge said, her voice no longer gentle. "Robert would have had to first get the gun, either from you or from Craig, and then return it to your room. Besides, the night Craig was murdered I heard Robert come in, and I heard him on his cell phone. With you, I understand, Hillary. Why did you ask him to come over and protect you when you already had three men in the condo with you? Was it so that he would be out of our condo at that particular time and you could make the accusation you just made?"

Hillary looked around the room as if seeking help.

"Looking for your next victim? I have to tell you, we have gone over everyone's movements thoroughly; I'm sure the police have, too. No one here had the opportunity or a motive strong enough to kill Craig—except for you. If you couldn't do it yourself, you had to get someone who loved you to do it for you. That would be Carmella."

Hillary turned to Robert, tears streaming out of wide blue eyes. "You promised your mother would help me. Why are you letting her say these awful things to me?"

Robert folded his arms across his chest. His eyes were sad but resigned as he looked at Hillary and shook his head. Marge could have applauded. Thank God her son wasn't dumb. Once his eyes were opened, he could see when he was being played.

"You had all these people trying to help you," Marge said. "Most of all, the woman who loved you enough to kill for you."

"*Woman* who loved me? Where did you get such a sick idea?" With jerky movements Hillary looked around the room again. She stopped and pointed. "Andrew," she said. "He hated Craig, and Craig took Carmella away from him. He didn't need any help. He did it all by himself."

"Shall we check with Richard to see if Andrew left the condo after Craig went out?" Marge asked. She knew Richard could have gone right to sleep, which would have allowed Andrew to get out without being seen or heard, but she hoped Hillary in her current state of mind wouldn't realize that.

Hillary's shoulders slumped. She closed her eyes and heaved a sigh, as if finally accepting the inevitable. "Well, then, Carmella must have done it. She wanted Craig. When she couldn't have him she must have gone crazy. Maybe she got the gun from Craig before we left Bellevue. And someone from our group must have been helping her and put it in my room, like you said."

Marge wished she had been looking at Carmella. She could feel the increase in tension in the air to her right. A glance at the detective assured her he had noted it, too; he had a better view than she did.

"Does Carmella know anyone else here?" Marge asked.

"Andrew." Hillary's voice was gaining in confidence.

Marge knew she had to be careful. She had to guard against asking any leading questions. The idea had to come from Hillary herself.

"Didn't she know all of you from office gatherings?"

"She met all of us, yes. But Andrew was the only one she knew. He was the only one who would do anything for her."

"Do anything? What do you mean?"

"Put the gun in my room. Run you down while Carmella was being questioned, in order to take suspicion away from her. Plant Anne's hair on my sweat suit and that pink hat in Anne's room."

The air to Marge's right was becoming absolutely frigid. She couldn't help another glance at the detective to make sure he was registering it. He was.

"But . . . I thought Carmella threw him over. Why would Andrew help her? And how would he get the key to her car?"

"He must still love her. He was always mooning about when she was at the office gatherings. They must have planned it together."

Marge frowned. "But why? What did either of them have to gain from Craig's death?"

"Don't you see?" It was difficult to recognize mousy little Hillary in the shrill voice and frantic movements. "Andrew got Carmella back. And Carmella got even with Craig for not leaving me and marrying her."

Marge turned slowly. The agonized look Carmella bestowed on Hillary stopped the words she was about to say.

"You fool," Carmella whispered, the bravado gone. "All you had to do was keep your mouth shut."

"So, you killed Craig for Hillary?"

Oops, Marge thought. Leading question.

Carmella continued to stare at Hillary as if seeing her for the first time. "Did you care for me at all," she finally whispered, "or did you just use me to get rid of Craig?"

There was no adoration in Hillary's eyes now. They were clear and hard. She had been an actress after all, fooling even Carmella with her act.

After another minute Carmella straightened her shoulders and turned to Marge. "No," she said. "I *would* have killed Craig for Hillary. I would have done anything for Hillary. I love . . . loved her. But I didn't kill Craig. Hillary said she had to kill Craig herself, for all that he had put her through."

Marge jerked upright. With so many crazy stunts to muddy the waters, she couldn't help think Carmella might be pulling another one.

"It was her." Hillary was pointing at Carmella and nearly shouting. "It was all her. She got the gun somehow. She followed him to Ocean Shores. She impersonated me on the beach to make me seem like a fake. She killed him. She got

Andrew to plant the gun in my room and to drive her car at you while she was in custody. It was all her."

Andrew broke in, his voice calm. "For the record, Andrew denies any involvement."

Marge ignored them both. "How did you make the timing work?" she asked Carmella. "Craig left Hillary at the condo. Was he shot on his way to your motel or on his return?"

"On the way back. I met him in the parking lot, took him into my room, and then goaded him into a fight. While I was doing that, Hillary snuck out and hid on the ledge above the driftwood. She left the gun there, along with the gloves she wore, in case she was seen returning to the condo. I got rid of the gloves and cleaned the gun before putting it in a place where she could find it when it was safe to take it back to her room."

"Then, you didn't get the gun from Hillary's purse at the holiday bazaar?" Marge asked.

Carmella gave a wry grin. "No, that was your imagination in overdrive," she said. When she looked at Hillary again, a range of emotions shifted across her face. Disbelief. Pain. Heartbreak. Resignation. Tears streaming, she turned to Detective Barker. "Please take me out of here. I'll tell you the whole truth."

"Don't believe her. She'll say anything," Hillary cried as Lieutenant Morgan and two uniformed officers entered the room and took both women into custody.

Hillary stopped and looked at Marge before they could hustle her out of the room. "You promised," she said in a low voice, worry shadowing her eyes. Marge knew she wasn't referring to the promise to Robert.

Marge nodded. "And I keep my promises," she said, "as long as I don't have to break the law to do it."

The Carmella being led away was a far different woman than the brash, assured Carmella. It was clear she was, or had been, in love with Hillary. Whatever she had done, she had done it for Hillary. And Hillary had used her.

Sweet little Hillary who wouldn't hurt a fly.

Realization of what had happened after the confession took a minute to sink in. Marge turned to Detective Barker, who was standing with Jane, casually sipping a beer. Marge's eyes widened when she saw Pete Peterson standing beside them. She frowned at Detective Barker. "You arranged for the county police to be here?" she asked.

"Yup."

"How did they know when to come in?"

Detective Barker grinned. "First time I ever got a chance to wear a wire."

"But . . . why? I mean, it was a good idea, but what made you decide to do it?"

"Oh, I don't know. I called your friend Pete again, after talking to you this morning. He thought you probably figured out who killed Carlson and had found a way to expose the culprit. He also warned I could be letting myself in for a ton of trouble if I participated in your little stunt and you were wrong, but that I should be prepared that you might be right. So I called the lieutenant to make sure I wasn't stepping on any toes. He agreed to oversee the whole thing. Not that he believed anything would come of it, but he was at a dead end so he had nothing to lose. At the least he said he could get a good laugh out of it."

"Pete," Marge said, "I thought you went back to Bellevue."

"I did," he said. "But when Detective Barker called me about your party tonight, I thought I'd like to attend. Unfortunately, the county police didn't let me listen in on the wire, so I don't know how it all went down."

"I think it's time for Jane and me to leave now," said Detective Barker. "We'll let Marge tell you all about it."

The detective's leaving seemed to open up the flood-gates.

"So, did Hillary do it? That's hard to believe. It must have been Carmella," Andrew exclaimed.

"I agree, Carmella would be more likely than Hillary to commit murder," Anne added.

"Lovers?" Robert almost whispered. He looked close to tears. "I was sure you were wrong, Mother. Couldn't there be some other explanation?"

Everyone looked uncomfortable.

"They weren't necessarily lovers, Robert," Andrew said. "I think Hillary was using Carmella; she may not have let it get that far. What surprises me is that someone as conniving as Hillary got trapped in a relationship with Craig."

"Oh, come on," Anne said. "You can't claim to know anything about Hillary and Carmella. After all, you dated Carmella and didn't figure out she was using you until she dumped you." She turned to Marge. "How did you ever figure it out?"

Marge shook her head and grinned. "A combination of that imagination on overdrive and my intuitive fingers," she said. "Obviously I didn't have it completely figured out. Hillary surprised me." She turned back to Pete. "Have you eaten anything? Do we have any food left?" It seemed like she always ended up feeding this detective.

Marge noticed that Andrew was watching her with a guarded expression. While Pete filled a plate, she walked over to him.

"So," Andrew said, "was I your vacation fling?"

"Was I yours?" she countered.

"I don't know. At first it seemed that way, but I was beginning to think we might have started something good." He glanced over at Pete. "If you aren't already involved we could find out."

Marge was silent for a long time, watching Pete as he talked with Robert. "I don't know if I'm involved or not," she said. "But I'm beginning to hope so. And you're too nice a guy to leave hanging, so I think we'll call this a good time while it lasted. You should have no trouble finding someone; in fact, I'm surprised you haven't already."

"That's because I wasn't looking," he said. "Being with you has made me realize there are good women out there and I'm missing out by not finding one for myself. So, maybe I'll see you around. Or maybe I'll start looking again."

Marge brushed her lips across his cheek and turned to find Pete watching her. She tried to ignore him as she walked over to talk with Robert.

"You okay?" she asked.

"I will be," he said. "I think I was shocked more than anything. Hillary had already pretty much brushed me off, so I knew there was no future in that relationship. I can't help but wonder why she asked me to come here at all, though. I don't think I did anything that helped her."

Marge drew him down in the biggest hug she could manage. "I think if you hadn't refused to run over here at her beckoning after you returned from Aberdeen, you would have been more useful to her. I don't know how she planned to kill Craig and keep you here at the same time, but thank God you didn't fall for it. When she got the idea to run at me with Carmella's car, she tried to set you up without an alibi for that time, too, since you also have a blue sedan. After that, she had no more need for you. It was a matter of keeping up a front and sending people off in different directions until she got out of here."

"How could I be so wrong about her? How can I ever trust my instincts about women?"

"You'll find the right person. Don't try to rush it." And this mother is ready to give it a helping hand, she thought.

Melissa came over. "Come on, Robert. Let's go back to Mariner Village."

"Wait, what about my ride?" Marge asked.

Melissa looked from Marge to Pete and ushered Robert out the door.

When Marge turned to see if she needed to help with cleaning up, Anne brushed her off. "You found out who killed Craig, and I'm grateful to you for that. I apologize for all my rudeness earlier."

Marge laughed. "I can be pretty pushy," she said. "I probably deserved it." She paused. "And, Anne, I hope you and John will consider marriage counseling before you call it quits. You've both had a lot of stress recently. Once you get past it, you may find you still have a marriage worth saving."

Anne looked at her for a long time. "Thanks," she finally said, "maybe we will do that."

Pete cleaned off his plate and came over to Marge. "How are you getting back to your condo?" he asked, his eyes on Andrew.

"I thought I'd walk," she said.

"I'll be driving right by it on my way to the motel," he said.

She let the silence linger.

"Want a ride?"

"I thought you'd never ask."

SIXTEEN

WHEN THEY ARRIVED at Mariner Village, Marge automatically reached for the car door. But it felt like the end of something, so she pulled her hand back. "Do you think the county police will let us know when they nail down all the details about what really happened?" she asked.

"I can probably find out, if you like," Pete said. "But at least you have the satisfaction that the guilty parties were caught." He grinned. "Even if you did create a slightly Agatha Christie-ish scene to do it."

"And, I saved Robert from getting involved with Hillary."

"Speaking of involvement," Pete said, turning to face Marge. She had to force herself to hold her head erect; it seemed to want to lean back on his arm, which extended over the back of her seat. "I think I owe you an apology."

Marge blinked and stared. Pete Peterson apologizing? "For what?" It took her a moment to realize she had spoken out loud.

"For stomping off yet again, the way I always do when you upset me. After I returned to my motel room and stewed for a while, I realized I had no business being upset. You had every right to see another man, even to have a relationship if it got that far. I certainly never told you . . . I'm uncomfortable saying anything now, but I promised myself I wouldn't keep things bottled up any longer."

Feeling Pete's discomfort, Marge got out of the car. When Pete followed, she led him toward the pool enclosure, stifling a desire to tell him it didn't make any difference. That it was all right. That she understood. Once out of the car, she had an equally strong desire to turn and run before he said something that could alter her life.

"You don't have to . . ."

"Don't stop me now. I need to say this," Pete said. "I care more about you than is comfortable, Marge Christensen, and it twists me up inside when I see you with another man. All I need from you, and you can take your time to answer me, is to know if there is any chance you might feel the same."

Marge felt paralyzed by the fear that gripped her. She had thought this was what she wanted, but she had promised herself never again to trust her happiness to another person. To give up her dreams for another person. Regardless of what Melissa said, didn't she risk that if she admitted to Pete what she felt?

"Take your time. I have to get back to Bellevue, but I didn't want to leave until I talked to you," Pete said. He turned to go back to the car.

"Wait," Marge cried. As torn as she felt, she knew she couldn't let Pete go without an answer. She reached out for his arm, but stopped. Suddenly nervous, she blurted, "At least you didn't storm out on me this time."

"No," he said. "No, I hope I never storm out on you again. If I'm upset I need to let you know, and tell you why. But I have no right to . . . expect anything from you."

Marge couldn't control the smile that grew on her face or the flutters she felt in her stomach. It would do her no good to try to play it cool now; her body was giving her away. She let her hand, still outstretched, touch his arm ever so gently. "I was afraid you had walked away for good. I didn't know what to do with the pain that idea caused. I do care about you, Pete Peterson. So much that it scares me."

As if pulled by a magnet, she stepped close to him and felt his arms encircle her. Leaning into the strength of his broad chest she knew the adolescent sparks she had felt with Kevin, the warmth she felt with Andrew, even the comfort she had felt with David, all combined in the way she felt now. Only there was so much more with Pete; she felt like this is where she belonged.

Panic gripped her. What was she doing? She had no idea what this would do to the life she had been building for herself. Would she have to give that up again?

Pete pulled her close and brought his lips down to meet hers, causing all sorts of wonderful feelings to course through her body. She knew it would be different this time. She wouldn't lose herself again. Except when she wanted to, she thought with a moan as she felt herself melt in his arms.

Pete's arms tightened around her for a moment before he grasped her shoulders and held her at arm's length. His gray eyes were lighter than Marge had ever seen them as he studied her face. They smiled at Marge before clouding with regret. "I really do have to go. I already missed one shift." He planted a soft kiss on the top of her head. "But, I'll be waiting for you to get home tomorrow."

Cold spread through Marge as he strode away. She leaned against the door and watched him go, savoring the memory of his strong arms holding her. Sighing, she opened the door.

Back to Bellevue tomorrow. Back to work and painting and art classes and worry about her children. Back to figuring out how she was going to do anything to help her mother in Michigan when her life was in Bellevue.

Especially now. Especially when she was going back to Detective Pete Peterson.

Was she ready?

Is this what she had been waiting for?

Don't miss the next Marge Christensen mystery . . .

Where Did You
MEET YOUR KILLER?

Turn the page for a preview . . .

Where Did You Meet Your Killer?

Three years have passed since Marge's vacation at Ocean Shores was disrupted by murder. Life in Bellevue is quiet and full. Her children are well, she is busy with painting, and even busier planning her upcoming wedding. Then she hears a breaking news report on the radio that there has been a homicide in Bellevue.

"Two weeks." Marge struggled to keep her voice from rising as she talked to Kate. "Two weeks before the wedding and someone has to go and get killed. What am I going to do?"

"Now, Mom," Kate's reasoning voice came across the line. "You have been in these situations before. In two weeks the murderer will probably be behind bars and everything will go on as planned."

"I have this awful feeling," Marge said, as she poured hot water over the herbal tea bag in her mug.

Kate knew exactly what her mother was talking about. "Mom, I don't see how you could be involved this time."

Marge thanked God for the wisdom He had endowed on her daughter—at least when it came to other people's lives.

"Thank you, Kate, that's just the common sense I need to hear right now."

Hanging up the phone, Marge cupped the mug in her hands and stepped onto her deck to look out over the multiple shades of green in Kelsey Creek Park. She took a deep breath and savored the freshness of the air after a mid-day rain.

The ringing of the telephone drew her back into the apartment. "Oh, Pete," she said as soon as she heard his voice. "I'm glad you called."

There was a moment of silence.

"Pete? Is something wrong?"

"This murder . . . the victim . . . ah, Marge. I'm sorry. It was Joshua. Your boss."

Marge felt a painful vise clamp her throat. For a moment she couldn't breathe. When the pressure became too much to stand, a sob escaped. "Joshua? How? When? Why? At the shop?"

"I wish I could have told you in person," Pete said, "but I can't get away right now and I didn't want you to learn about it on the news." Marge heard a voice in the background call out to Pete. "I have to go, but I phoned Melissa and she should be there any minute."

Marge was at her open apartment door with one arm tight across her stomach and one hand clamped over her mouth when Melissa arrived. Melissa pulled her friend back into the apartment, closed the door, and wrapped Marge in her arms.

"Oh, Marge, I'm so sorry."

Marge hiccoughed through her sobs. "Who would want to hurt that gentle old man?" she stammered.

"That's what Pete is going to find out."

ABOUT THE AUTHOR

PATRICIA K. BATTA, a Michigan native, attended Northwestern Michigan Community College in Traverse City, received her B.A. from the University of Puerto Rico, and finished at Oberlin College in Ohio with a Master's Degree in education.

Batta has been writing since she was ten years old. By the time she retired, she had drafted two mystery novels and was working on a third.

She lives in Traverse City, where she is active in her church, the Love INC organization, and writing.

You may contact her via www.lillimarpublishing.com or www.patriciabatta.blogspot.com.